Red-Tailed Hawk

Nancy Schoellkopf

Cover design by Karen Phillips

Author photo by Leslie Rose, cropping by John Crandall

RED-TAILED HAWK

Nancy Schoellkopf

For my mother
Bernice Schoellkopf

whose support gave me the courage
to pursue my dreams.

Chapter One

In this neighborhood bordered by interstate freeways and snow-fed rivers, the trees are so dense that a hawk or hummingbird flying over it may mistake this urban landscape for an orchard. In summer and fall the tips of the leaves wink and flutter like water rippling on the surface of a large rectangular lake. In winter the sky is filled with bare bones, knobby and aching. Looking down, the crosshatched grid of numbered and lettered streets is unsheltered and the pavement is cold.

But in spring fresh buds crack open and new leaves perch on their stems like stiff feathers, beckoning all those with wings to come home.

In a season such as this the valley air often feels heavily dusted and sleepy, but on this particular Saturday, midnight rain had washed away pollen and mold spores. Overladen camellia bushes had dropped rust-tipped blossoms during the storm. Flowers still on the stem looked moist and heavy.

Treading lightly over fallen petals, an auburn haired girl walked down a sidewalk cracked with sycamore roots and wild chamomile. Her name was Mariah Easter and she was seventeen years old. Her breasts were still hard and her hips boyish, but her soft brown eyes were deep set and ancient-looking, tinged with amber like a cat's. She stepped quietly as if unwilling to leave evidence of her presence. She carried a wallet, a canvas shopping bag, and a hollow ache between her belly and the spot where her ribs flared together. This emptiness was a constant companion, like a caged bird that occasionally stretched its wings, flapping in frustration.

This morning she was on a quest seeking Cherry Garcia ice cream. It was her mother's birthday, and her father was cooking a special dinner. Mariah would bake a cocoa fudge cake. The ice cream had to be Mom's favorite. That was the kind of touch her father wouldn't think of.

Her first attempt was the Mom and Pop Market at 24th & N Streets. They didn't have any. So she walked five blocks west and five blocks south to the Safeway with the big silver horse sculpture out front. Plenty of frozen desserts to choose from there. She bought two pints of the Ben and Jerry's treat, then gave her last dollar to a scruffy bearded man in army fatigues begging at the south exit.

Mariah was grateful for a quiet winter weekend at home with her parents. She had begged off invitations to parties and basketball games. Her boyfriend Todd had suggested movies and concerts, but Mariah knew all dates led to the back seat of Todd's Toyota Corolla. *Is this what it means to be an adult?* she wondered. *A woman at ease with new experiences? With adventure?*

Heading home to their bungalow at the bottom of the hill, Mariah slung her canvas bag casually over her shoulder. She knew she would not mind missing the usual weekend gatherings of her school friends at a coffee house or pizza parlor. Talk swirled around impending graduation and college plans. Most of her friends were hot to leave town, half because they wanted to break loose from parental shackles, the rest because they were blessed to have already mapped plans to meet specific career goals. Mariah envied them their focus.

She herself was opting to stay at home this coming fall with Mom and Dad, to attend the local state college minutes from their home via the light rail train. Friends challenged her to join them in southern California or on the east coast, and Mariah wondered at her own reluctance. She had a connection here, not only to her family, but also to this place: the urban pulse, the marriage of two rivers, the redwood planted in their backyard, its branches draped protectively above her bedroom window. Still she had to ask: was she too comfortable here?

She knew her mother did not intend to be dismissive, but she repeatedly told Mariah that she was young, and "I promise you'll know what to do when the time is right." Her father said, "It is never about doing, Mariah. It is about being."

Mariah wanted to tell her parents about her deep yearning for something she couldn't name, but she didn't have the words. How could this emptiness be filled? Mariah didn't know, but she suspected that eventually some action, some "doing" would be required.

Waiting for the light to change at the corner of 19th and T Streets, Mariah breathed deeply and deliberately to banish anxious thoughts about the future. She silently chanted a few lines from the Angelus, a prayer her mother had taught her. Traffic stopped. She crossed the street, swinging her bag rhythmically at her side.

The street was empty as she passed McClatchy Library. *Whoosh!* A gusty exhalation disturbed the still air: she felt its gentle movement against her hair and eyelashes. A large bird sailed above her head. His wingspan was broad, four feet at least. His under belly was downy and light, the color of creamy latte.

Mariah watched as the bird lit in the branches of a plane tree forty feet or more above the ground. She could see his hooked beak, his outward-searching eyes. The hawk leaned forward; he was watching her too. They made eye contact, held each other's gaze.

Mesmerized, Mariah took a step forward. The bird didn't flinch. She inched closer. His head bobbed, encouraging. She dared a third step, and the hawk lifted its head, spread its wings and launched itself into the sky. It swept above her, then circled to soar away.

***

A few blocks east, the sun was casting rainbows on soap bubbles as Charlie Easter dipped a towel into a bucket of cold soapy water, then splashed it down on the hood of his wife's car. Samantha was off having brunch with a friend. Finding a clean car in the garage when she got home would be a happy surprise.

Charlie imagined for a moment that he might blow the foam into the air and each wayward bubble would turn into a black-chinned hummingbird. He could hear the abrupt metallic clicks of a hummingbird now, fueling his fantasy with the "stit stit stit" of its chase call. They sounded like wind-up toys, surprisingly loud these deceptive birds, tiny but fierce. He turned to search, finding one deep in the foliage of a camellia bush heavy-laden with passionate red blossoms. He stared at the creature, feeling again the presence of invisible cities, here in the moist soil of his back yard, providing shelter for his fears, his memories and every mythic animal that had ever visited him whether on earth plane or dreamscape.

The hummingbird took flight, zipping past him with the flash and speed of a laser pointer. He thought of his first lover--his son's mother Geneva: she was like that when they were young. She was a wild bird, beautiful and in a great hurry. Samantha was beautiful too, but she had a rooted energy like that of a nesting robin. No, wait—Sam wasn't the robin, she was the tree--a valley oak-- where the robin would feel safe building its nest. For Charlie, Geneva had been a quick trip up a steep mountain and back again. But Sam was his sanctuary. Look how she had tamed him: here he was washing her car on a Saturday morning. A few years ago he would have wanted to hitchhike to the coast, seeking a glimpse of hard granite and black ocean, a landscape reminiscent of his boyhood in New

England. Raised amid such stark beauty, a child couldn't help but grow into a man who was direct and harsh. But now, dwelling with Sam near a river, a cottony landscape softened with tule rushes and the scent of fennel, he had acquired a bit of patience. What's more, he had come to see the virtues of a California winter. It was invigorating in its briskness here, sure, but still warm enough to please his aging muscles and ligaments. At sixty-two, he had more aches and pains than he'd care to admit to his wife. Fifty-plus years of pickup basketball and rock climbing had taken a toll on his hips, knees and lower back. He still had a full head of hair, though his once dark locks were now a mixture of gray and white.

He was working his way to the back of the car when he saw his teenaged daughter running toward him on the sidewalk. For a split second his heart was in his throat: why was she running? Was she okay? Was something wrong? And again this omnipresent fear he had that some harm would befall her pushed its way to the surface, shooting a quick jolt of adrenaline into his solar plexus. He froze a moment, horrified that he had allowed the unspeakable into his consciousness, when unbidden, a new thought occurred: what if he weren't here to protect her?   What would happen then?   And immediately he knew he must speak to his son, Mariah's half brother, now nearly twice her age. He had to have this conversation with Dale, ask him to take care of his stepmother and half sister if--well, just if.

But now he could see that Mariah was smiling and waving, shouting to him, "Daddy!" The burst of adrenaline spilled into his heart and he remembered the evening eighteen years ago when he returned to California from an extended trip back east to discover his lover was four months pregnant. The instant surrender: he would never regret it.

"Wha-cha got?" he called to her, motioning with his chin toward her tote bag.

"Later--I'll tell you later." Panting a bit from her sprint, she threw herself into his arms, kissed his cheek and then bounced back, her face beaming, her hands gesturing with excitement. "I saw this huge hawk! Right here in the city--in midtown-- two blocks up the street!"

"Must have been a red-tail," he said quickly and he saw her frown. What? He pressed his lips together. Her mother did this too. Hated to be interrupted. Wanted her moment in the spotlight--a monologue, not a dialogue. "Red-tails are the ones you see most often in the city," he said in an apologetic tone.

She pushed strands of her auburn hair off her forehead. "The hawk and I," she was saying softly. "We had this moment. He looked at me, he was looking right at me."

Charlie dropped his towel into the bucket. Mariah, he knew, was a child of nature, just as he himself was. He had seen her fascination with birds and bugs, with the raccoons and opossums that occasionally haunted their backyard. She had a special connection with animal spirits: he could see it! This gave him hope: he wanted her to tread a path of wild and sacred potential. He wanted the earth to be her ally. He did not want her to define herself by her wounds. Her mother did that. Well, he had to admit it: so did he.

Mariah was looking up now, reliving her mystical moment. "He was so high above the ground," she said, "but I could see he was looking right into my eyes."

"They have very keen eyesight," Charlie interjected and this time Mariah didn't frown. She nodded and smiled wistfully.

"It's as if we came to an understanding," she continued in her slow steady way. "Some kind of an agreement."

Charlie smiled. "An agreement? About what?"

"I don't know yet," she laughed, looking a little embarrassed, but Charlie knew it was no joke. He reached his arm around her and pulled her close again. "Well, you keep me posted, okay?"

***

The Easter family lived in a 1920s bungalow at the bottom of the neighborhood's only hill, a gentle rise dubbed Poverty Ridge. Back in Gold Rush days, long before levees were built to tame the wild waters, before the sidewalks were raised to create a reliable city infrastructure, washed-out miners and shopkeepers would come to this high ground with their few salvaged possessions to camp when the mountain snows melted, forcing rivers to rush and meander across the valley floor. This is the city the Spanish named for the Blessed Sacrament, though Samantha O'Malley Easter did not know why. She had been born here, and she felt blessed that she found her way back every time she dared to wander away.

Tonight she sat in the back yard at dusk, waiting for the first star of the evening to appear. She leaned back in a sturdy wooden lawn chair, delighted at how long the days were growing, realizing that it would be the equinox in less than a week. She and Charlie had bought this house together eighteen years ago this month. She remembered sitting out here in this very chair, her feet elevated on a bucket, big as a house, pregnant with Mariah. Charlie had crouched nearby, clearing a space to plant a mandarin orange. The tree had been labeled a dwarf, but it defiantly grew. Now it towered over the fence.

Samantha's normally manic husband promised her a quiet day and he had delivered: there was no surprise party, no outing to a crowded concert hall or bar, no trip to a busy shopping mall for a surprise spending spree in her honor. Charlie had even suggested—since he and Mariah planned to spend a good portion of the day sequestered in the kitchen— that Samantha head out to a restaurant with her friend Craig.

Craig had been the night custodian in the first school where Samantha taught special education. Back then she was deeply depressed, working with a bullying principal and uncooperative assistants, but Craig swooped in to pick her up, hold her hand and see her through.

Though he did not practice religious rituals or attend a church, Samantha knew Craig was a holy man who had a special relationship with the Divine. He often seemed to know what people were thinking before they voiced it themselves, but he would not allow Samantha to call him a psychic. He occasionally could foresee events before they occurred, but he would not claim the title of clairvoyant. He was a big bear of a man with shiny pate and laughing Buddha bearing. He'd been Charlie's buddy, Mariah's godfather, and Samantha's best friend for nearly three and a half decades.

Lunch with Craig meant sharing pork chow mein and pork ribs with the paradoxically uber-carnivorous spiritual master. Tucked into a back booth they meditated and shared poetry between courses, then Samantha had a scoop of green tea ice cream while Craig ordered more pot stickers.

"I wish I could retire at the end of this semester," Samantha confided to Craig. "But I think it'll be a few more years before I can afford to do that."

Craig sipped his soda. "Talk to your financial advisor. You may be able to do that sooner than you think."

Samantha sat up and leaned forward. Craig made few predictions anymore, but when he did Samantha always listened. "Why do you say that?"

"I don't know," he said, gazing past her, above her right shoulder. "I feel you're going to have more time to spend with Mariah. I see the two of you by the riverbank, looking at birds with binoculars. And Mariah catches sight of a hawk. A big hawk, circling slowly above the cottonwood trees." He paused to look at her face. "You know the ones that grow down near the bike trail."

Samantha pulled back at the image. Years ago, before Mariah was born, Samantha had seen a hawk kill a tiny sparrow. It was a chilling sight, and she hadn't thought about it in years. "Mariah and a hawk," she mused. "That sounds ominous."

"Oh, no," Craig assured her. "Hawks are powerful, mystical birds. A time is coming when Mariah will seek out new mentors who will lead her where she needs to go."

Samantha grasped her water glass, but she didn't drink from it. She felt a need to hold something cool, something grounding—if you could call water grounding. She sighed audibly, and Craig grinned at her. He had the most joyful smile of anyone she had ever seen. His entire jaw fanned with laugh lines and his eyes and forehead crinkled. "You worry too much!" he exclaimed, shaking his head, as if her melancholy sigh were a wonderfully crafted and hilarious pun.

She snorted indignantly as if to prove her resilience. "I guess I thought that you'd be her mentor--the way you've always been mine."

"I'll do what I can for her," he said shortly. "But the time will come--perhaps sooner than we expect--when we both may be asking her to mentor us!"

Samantha came home to a house warm with the scent of tomato sauce and chocolate. Charlie had made a luscious veggie lasagna, using spinach and broccoli from the back yard patch. Mariah had baked a cocoa fudge cake--a recipe Samantha's mother used to bake for her birthday way back when she was a little girl. Mariah had found the recipe last summer when she was leafing through Samantha's jumbled collection of cookbooks seeking a recipe for lemon bars. "Maybe I'll be a pastry chef some day," Mariah had announced as she brought in the heaping bowls of cake topped with Ben and Jerry's ice cream.

"I think you'd be good at that," Samantha was quick to tell her daughter, and she meant it. Mariah put so much heart into the meals she made, and she seemed so focused and carefree when she was in the kitchen. Not the way Samantha herself went about the task of cooking dinner: dashing about, head bowed over cutting board and stove burners, intent on finishing up this tedious task as quickly as possible. Charlie's style was decidedly different, but not much better. He meandered around the kitchen in an almost aimless manner, nibbling as he went, stopping for long breaks to wash some-- but not all--the dishes, and then to read the sports section or a chapter of a text book for whatever class he was subbing in. Maybe he'd take a taste, try a few spices, then grab a notebook to dash off a few lines of poetry. Samantha often got impatient when it was Charlie's turn to cook. Sometimes she gave up waiting and made a meal of sliced cucumber and hummus as she wrote lesson plans for her special education class.

Mariah beamed at her mother's affirmation. "Do you like the cake?" she asked. "Is it as good as you remember?"

"Better," Samantha crooned as she filled her mouth with a hefty bite of butter cream frosting and ice cream. "So good."

"It's kind of dense," Charlie complained, and Samantha kicked him under the table.

"Oh, Daddy," Mariah lamented. "You don't like it?"

Samantha swallowed quickly. "Charlie, it's supposed to be this way!" she scolded. "Rich and chocolaty!"

"Oh, well, it is that," he amended. "Can't fault the flavor. It's delicious."

Mariah looked relieved, though not completely convinced. "It's great if you eat it in really thin slices," Samantha added. "Though your grandmother liked big chunky pieces just like these!" She took another bite as Charlie rose. "Are you done already?" she asked.

"No," he said simply. "I'm getting seconds."

Mariah grinned at her mother. "Guess it wasn't too bad," she whispered and they had both laughed quietly.

Samantha smiled as she remembered the satisfied look on Mariah's face. But her smile faded as she glanced at the veggie patch and flower garden. The broccoli was getting sparse and the pansies and cyclamen were nearly spent. She and Charlie needed to do some weeding and clearing, maybe work some mulch into the soil in preparation for summer tomatoes and squash. She sighed. She was a woman obsessed with to-do lists and schedules. Craig had said as much to her today when she complained of increasing paperwork at school. "How you do anything is how you do everything," he quoted.

"What?" she had asked, squinting in confusion.

"An old Buddhist saying: it means taste your ice cream! You're so busy worrying about work that you're off in your head someplace. Come back here. Be in this moment. Taste your ice cream!"

She looked up then to see the first tiny light flicker on in the gray-blue blanket of sky. The light had an orange tinge. It wasn't a star at all; it was probably Mars. *No matter,* Samantha thought. *It'll do.* She closed her eyes and made a wish. Sure, she was a pragmatic woman, but she had a fervent belief in the power of prayer, wishes, and ritual. And these days, all her wishes were for Mariah.

She went inside to prepare for bed. On this her 60th birthday, she'd had myriad reminders of mortality. Confronting herself in the mirror as she brushed her teeth, she encountered a few more. Her long chestnut hair was streaked with white, yet she refused to cut or color it. Her mouth was pinched with years of pressing and puckering her lips in anxiety and worry. But her eyes were accentuated with laugh lines. Signs of a balanced life, she decided.

She stepped back then and noticed her own posture. She held her elbow up even with her mouth, her arm awkwardly bent at a ninety-degree angle, frantically jerking her whole arm back and forth to move the brush in her mouth, faster, faster, faster. Let's get this thing over with. No time to waste brushing your teeth for crying out loud!

How you do anything is how you do everything, Craig had told her—and he was right.

She spat in the sink and rinsed her mouth out with water. Quickly. She rinsed off her brush, slapped it into a cup in the cabinet and then hastened out of the bathroom.

Charlie sprawled on the large bed he shared with his wife, waiting for her to come out of the bathroom. He was feeling smugly satisfied at how well the evening had gone, and he couldn't help but wonder if he could persuade Samantha to enhance her birthday celebration a bit further. He yawned and stretched, reminding himself to let the evening evolve. He saw a fresh book of haiku on Samantha's nightstand. Wondering if it was a birthday present, he rolled onto her side of the bed. He was reaching for the book when Samantha slid the bathroom door open and strode into the room. "Have you brushed your teeth yet?" she asked him.

"No. Why?"

"I don't know," she said, seeming distracted. "I wanted to watch and see how you brush your teeth."

He sat up and raised an amused eyebrow at her. "Well, that's a new one," he said in a suggestive tone. "Kind of kinky, even for you Ms Omm."

He saw her smile reluctantly at the old reference, and he

had to laugh. He used to call her that when they first met, when she was known school wide as Ms O'Malley. O-M for O'Malley, slurred into Omm because she liked to meditate.

"Never mind, Mystery," she retorted, resorting to an equally old nickname she had for him, based on blending Mister E--for Mr. Easter--into a very apt moniker, Mystery.

She sat down next to him on the bed. He leaned toward her, angling for a kiss, but she didn't seem to notice. Grabbing a bottle of lotion she began to smooth cream onto her shins and knees. He sat back against the pillows and exhaled. "You know, Sam, I've been wanting to ask you something," he said. "Do you ever worry about Mariah?"

She turned toward him quickly. "Why?" she asked, sounding frantic at the suggestion. "Is something wrong?"

"No, nothing really." He paused and she stared at him intently until he began to wonder if he was growing potato eyes on his face. He rubbed his chin and shrugged. "I don't know," he said finally. "I guess it's that she's getting older.

Samantha turned her attention back to her dry heel. "Well, I can't say I like that boy she's seeing too much."

"You don't like Todd?" Charlie asked, surprised. "Why not? He's a Pats fan."

Samantha looked up from her parched left knee. "Oh, Charlie, he's no more a New England Patriots fan than I am! He's kissing up to his girlfriend's father."

Charlie felt slapped. "What are you saying? You don't like the Pats?"

Samantha rolled her eyes. "That's the big take-away here?" she asked. "Jeez, Charlie." She took a deep breath. "You know, I like 'em all right, but I'm no big fan."

Charlie jumped up and paced at the foot of the bed. "It's

like I don't even know you!" He watched her laugh at his hyperbole as he knew she would, so he continued to shake his head in mock shock. "You cut me to the quick, woman," he said, unable to hide a grin.

"Get back on task, Easter," she volleyed back, affecting her teacher demeanor. "Why are you worried about Mariah?"

He shrugged, feeling a bit subdued yet grateful that she always brought him back on point. He stretched out next to her, but still couldn't find the words. "It was nothing," he told her.

Now she looked annoyed. "Why can't I believe you? Charlie?--c'mon, what is it?"

He returned her gaze for a moment, finally licking his lips. "So-- you don't like Todd?" She rolled her eyes, but he pressed on. "Okay no more joking," he said. "I didn't know. Is there something I should know about Todd?"

She shrugged, staring at her hands. "I have a feeling about him. I think he takes advantage of her."

Charlie rolled onto his back, wondering for the first time if his daughter was sleeping with her boyfriend. He felt his throat constrict, but he knew he had to be patient, had to feel this frantic emotion, this loss of control, let it rock him and release him. If it was true, he hoped she was safe, he hoped she felt some joy in it. *Todd is not worthy of her:* the thought came to him unbidden but he knew he was not resentful or biased. Charlie liked Todd well enough, but he knew Todd could not keep up with Mariah. Mariah was sharp as a whip. She had her mother's patience and creativity, and she had her father's curiosity. For if there was one indisputable fact Charlie knew about himself, it was this: he was a seeker—and so was Mariah. If she were like him, she would feel compelled to gather knowledge from all kinds of people and places and books. When he was younger he treasured above all else his freedom to pick up and go traveling when his feet got itchy.

Now he had to remind himself—sometimes several times a day—that his journey hadn't ended, it had merely turned within. He had committed himself to one bed and one woman. This was his path now.

He stared at the ceiling wishing he could somehow convey the great rush of emotion he felt watching their daughter run down the hill toward him that morning. How happy he felt to know that she belonged to them, but no, didn't belong to them. She didn't, did she? Not anymore. But she had been theirs. They had created her together. It was all so sappy, but definitely genuine. "I was watching Mariah this morning," he started slowly. "She was walking down the sidewalk toward me and it struck me how grown up she's getting to be and--I don't know—there's something so magical about her--"

Samantha snuggled down next to her husband. "Of course there is," she said gently. "She's *your* daughter."

He smiled at that, feeling appeased. Yet he felt Sam didn't quite understand. He needed to warn her. How could he articulate this vague concern that Mariah might somehow be spirited away by a hawk? It was absurd, he knew it was, but he could see a path opening before her. It was a path he himself would never be able to resist. And as Sam had just pointed out, she was *his* daughter.

"I know it's selfish," Samantha said as if reading his mind, "but I can't help but wish that we could freeze time so she'd stay our little girl forever."

Charlie turned to look into her eyes. "I love both of you so much, Sam."

She touched his cheek. "I know," she whispered. He leaned in to kiss her. She sighed and opened her mouth to let him inside.

Later Samantha padded down the hall to check on her daughter, to see if she was still up reading or drawing or talking on Facebook. The bathroom door was ajar and she glanced in to see Mariah brushing her teeth. She brushed slowly and deliberately, her gaze focused on her mouth in the mirror, her body swaying gently as if she were chanting.

Chapter Two

The kitchen was the largest room in the Easter household and it was indisputably Charlie's domain. Though Samantha routinely dished up every-day fare like Cheerios with bananas or scrambled eggs for breakfast, as well as portable lunches of healthy salads and sandwiches, at dinner Charlie took the stage like an artist in his studio, transforming potatoes, cheese, fish, chicken or rice into delectable concoctions with generous splashes of fresh lemon juice or sauces created with coconut milk or tomatoes.

Most afternoons, Mariah loyally camped at the kitchen table, ostensibly toiling at her homework, but watching as her father trimmed fresh herbs trailing from pots on the windowsills, feeling bemused as he sauntered in from the yard, his arms heavy with carrots and squash from the garden. When she was little, she loved to sketch crayoned drawings of the still life arrangements Charlie had inadvertently assembled on the counter: sprigs of mint, bottles of Paul Newman's salad dressing and bumpy bits of ginger root. Later, in her teens, she tried to take notes as he cooked, hoping to hit pay dirt and capture a recipe or two that would be worth repeating. But Charlie's dishes were always one of a kind, appearing on their dining room table to make a debut and a finale at one and the same time, a creation so spontaneous that it couldn't be re-created if he tried. Charlie would laugh about this. "Don't you see, Mariah?" he'd say. "This meal reflects the precious and temporal nature of life itself!" Samantha was resigned to her husband's quirky stubbornness. "He cooks the way he lives," she'd tell her daughter. "He follows the energy and there's nothing I can do to change him. I stopped trying to tame him long ago."

But Samantha would never trust Charlie's energetic approach to holiday fare. After all on an average Tuesday or Friday night, if Charlie's impromptu meal proved unpalatable, Samantha could call Zelda's or Los Jarritos and the family could get deep-dish pizza or Mexican take-out within a half hour. But on Thanksgiving and Christmas, Samantha believed it was the task of the cook to preserve a matrilineal legacy of family recipes and traditions. No experimental oysters or chestnuts in her turkey dressing, no horseradish in her potatoes. She had a civilization to maintain.

So it was surprising to Charlie and Mariah when Samantha announced her plan to deviate from their usual Easter ham so she could roast a leg of lamb. She was eager to teach Mariah a nearly forgotten technique her mother had shown her decades ago.

"You have to be sure your knife is sharp," she told Mariah as she sliced a tiny X in the flesh of the meat. Then she inserted a clove of garlic into the deep pocket of the X. "That's all there is to it!"

"Oh, let me try," Mariah said, and Samantha gratefully handed off the knife. She stood back to watch as Mariah tattooed a tapestry of X's across the raw lamb. Samantha was pleased. It was a small thing, and easy too, but it felt like a sacred ritual she was handing down to her daughter, like following a knitting pattern or praying the mysteries of the rosary.

Samantha was peeling more garlic when she heard Charlie call to her from the dining room where he was reading the Sunday paper. "Sam." His voice sounded so nonchalant she would tell people later. So easy going and soft.

"Yeah, Babe?" she answered.

"Sam," he said again.

"What, Charlie?"

"Sam," he said a third time.

"Something's wrong," Mariah said and she put down the knife.

Samantha gave her daughter's shoulder a reassuring squeeze. Mariah was so like her, worrying all the time. She eased past her and leaned out the kitchen door. "Wha--" But she couldn't even finish this one syllable word. Charlie was on his knees, one hand clutching his chest, the other gripping the table leg attempting to stay upright. His jaw was clenched and his eyes were pressed shut. His throat looked blue.

"Charlie!" she heard her voice squeal, then somehow she was at his side, though she didn't remember walking there. She pawed helplessly at his shoulder. "Can you get up?" she asked.

"Just call," he said.

Samantha jumped up, but Mariah was already on the other side of the room, speaking into the phone.

"Chest pains," she was saying. "My father can't move--it's so bad."

He was on his back now, swaying from side to side. Then he wasn't.

Hours later at the hospital, Samantha sat on a couch in the hallway. Mariah lay crumpled and sobbing in her lap. Samantha lifted her hand and began wiping her wet eyes with her fingers. She could still smell the garlic cloves. The clove itself doesn't have that mouth-watering scent of garlic bread or garlic infused pasta. It has a raw naked scent, the scent she'd known ever since her mother taught her how to cut the little holes in the meat and stick the cloves inside. It didn't remind her of garlic. It reminded her of dead flesh.

***

Samantha settled herself next to Mariah in the limousine. Mariah was wearing a summery, cotton sundress, and it was only now, on their way to the funeral, that Samantha wondered at the appropriateness of this choice. The ivory dress had a gathered bodice that revealed Mariah's budding cleavage, yet her bony shoulders and wrists displayed a lingering fragility. Samantha ran a protective hand across her daughter's full lacy skirt. Mariah leaned her head against her mother's shoulder. Samantha sighed. It was way too late for her to be questioning Mariah's attire.

She herself was wearing a pale linen skirt she reserved for meetings with parents and administrators, though she'd paired it with an embroidered turquoise blouse that Charlie had given her last Christmas. "I love your California style," Charlie's sister Hyacinth had greeted her that morning. "So casual and fresh!" She'd leaned in to finger Samantha's collar as if straightening it, but Samantha suspected Hyacinth was checking to see if the fabric was silk or polyester.

Hyacinth had flown out from Connecticut, arriving mid-afternoon the day after Charlie died, bearing luggage and laptop, a case of French wine and a carton filled with old family photo albums. She had worn nothing but black all week: black jacket and skirt, black pants with a black silk twin set, and for bed an oversized black T shirt and black yoga pants. Samantha wondered if this was her official mourning wardrobe or if black was simply de rigueur among her east coast social set.

Hyacinth was thinner than the last time Samantha had seen her, and certainly taller than she remembered. Her long limbs seemed reluctant to bend, keeping her at arm's length from the dinner table, her computer keyboard and of course anyone whose hand she deigned to shake. She had a husky voice, what Samantha's mother used to call a "whiskey and cigarette" voice. Samantha chalked this up to what Charlie had dubbed her "diva years" singing torch songs at Greenwich Village nightclubs after giving up on her dream of becoming an opera soprano. Later she married into a moneyed family of lawyers and stock brokers, finding her true calling on the boards of some of the biggest charities in NYC. After her divorce she had retreated home to New Haven where she busied herself raising money for her two alma maters, Choate/Rosemary Hall and the Yale Music Department.

Samantha glanced over at her in the limousine. She wore a stunning black suit with black satin shell. Her head was bowed, her right hand lifted to cup the headset in her right ear as she conferred in a low modulated voice with the caterer.

Hyacinth had an authoritative air that Samantha could only envy. Within minutes of arrival she was peppering Samantha with questions about the funeral arrangements, pulling an iPad from her large leather tote to craft an action plan. Samantha had glanced frantically around the room, but she was alone with her sister-in-law. Charlie's son Dale had graciously delivered Hyacinth from the airport, but he and Mariah had disappeared into a back bedroom, lugging their aunt's assortment of suitcases. At that moment, Samantha's friend Craig rang the front door bell as if summoned, though his visit was pre-arranged. He had offered to cut the lawn so it would look presentable for the post-funeral reception.

"That woman wants to take over everything!" Samantha blurted as she darted onto the front porch with Craig.

"Well," Craig responded, comically assuming Samantha's indignant tone, "if Charlie's sister thinks she can waltz in here and take over everything, well, then--you should let her!" Samantha looked up at him stunned. "Samantha," he said gently. "You've been fighting for the inclusion of your special ed students for so long that you've forgotten it's okay to surrender sometimes. If she wants to be in charge, let her be in charge. It's how she copes."

Craig was the only person whose advice Samantha had come to trust with little to no protest. She often called him her spiritual guide, but he always scoffed. "You don't need a guide," he'd say sternly. "You are your own guide." Samantha liked to think this was true, but she was grateful for his strong arm to lean on. She immediately conceded that where Hyacinth was concerned, Craig was right.

By the time Samantha returned to the house, Hyacinth had hired a caterer, a house cleaning service, and a pianist to play at the service. Samantha sighed deeply and thanked Hyacinth for her initiative. But when Hyacinth began to outline plans to have Charlie's body flown back east to be interred in the Easter family plot, Samantha put her foot down. "Charlie was my husband, and he will lie next to me here in California, in a Catholic cemetery," she said softly. Dale had emerged then to prove he had Samantha's back. "Remember, Aunt Hy, my sister and I are native Californians. The Easter family has a west coast branch now. We want our father's body here—at home with us."

Hyacinth's mouth pinched into a tense knot, but she said nothing more on this subject. Immediately she had turned her iPad to display an improvised floor plan rearranging Samantha's living room furniture to make way for a buffet line and additional tables. Dale had sat down with her then and calmly navigated through each minute detail of the funeral to come. Samantha sat across from them, holding her head and trying to stay awake.

***

Hyacinth looked up now to bestow what Samantha had come to recognize as her warm smile. "All systems go!" she whispered as she removed the ear bud. Samantha sighed in relief. She's been worried Hyacinth would wear the headset throughout the entire mass.

Despite her stiff, all-business demeanor, Hyacinth had unintentionally managed to endear herself to Samantha. It had happened after Dale had left, when Hyacinth finally set aside her computer to crack open one of her many travel bags. She extracted three pastel-colored boxes: a flat and rectangular baby blue box, a cube-shaped pale yellow box, and a tiny lavender box like those that hold rings or brooches. "I'm rather tired," she said to Samantha as she set the containers on Samantha's dining room table. "Jet lag, you know. But before I retire, I have a bit of a presentation I'd like to make."

Initially Samantha felt annoyed. She'd seen plenty of attention seeking behavior during her years in special ed— most often from parents and administrators. Why this theatricality? She forced a smile. "This is very kind of you, Hyacinth, but it wasn't necessary to bring gifts."

Hyacinth raised her hand to quell Samantha's protest. "These," she began haltingly, "are special. They're for Mariah. Family heirlooms from her grandmother and great grandmother."

Hyacinth looked into Samantha's eyes and Samantha could see vulnerability and sadness there. Craig had urged Samantha to surrender, but now Samantha sensed she was witnessing a true release by her sister-in-law. Hyacinth had had no children of her own. With the death of her only sibling it seemed she was letting go of any hope for another heir. "I'll get Mariah," she said.

She found Mariah in the back yard, literally crying on her godfather's shoulder. Craig reached out his other arm to Samantha, and she gratefully allowed him to enfold her as well. "Come inside with me," she said.

Samantha and Craig followed Mariah into the dining room. "You are so generous to think of me, Auntie Hy!" Mariah said, embracing her aunt. Samantha gripped Craig's wrist when she saw Hyacinth grimace, apparently averse to such physical affection. She lowered her eyes, embarrassed for her sister-in-law.

"Oh, please, Mariah," Hyacinth said quickly, "please sit down and allow me to gift you with these small keepsakes."

Mariah obediently sat in her usual place at the family table. Samantha sat across from her, deliberately choosing Charlie's chair. Craig stood behind Samantha, his hands hovering near her shoulders.

Hyacinth chose the long flat box first. "Here you go, dear," she said with no further ceremony.

"Thank you," Mariah said, smiling at her mother and godfather as she lifted the lid of the blue box. Inside, wrapped in ivory colored tissue paper was a dresser set--a silver plated brush, comb and mirror with the initial M engraved on the mirror and brush. "Why they even have my initial on them!" Mariah exclaimed.

"Oh, a very lucky coincidence," Hyacinth noted. "Your grandmother's name was Melora--so you share the M."

"Oh, but Daddy always said there are no coincidences!" Mariah blurted. Samantha pressed her lips together hoping she wouldn't be forced to explain the New Age philosophies Charlie Easter lived by.

"How very interesting," Hyacinth said with a twist of her head. "Must be a Californian idea."

"Well, I'm sure Charlie would say that this stunning dresser set was destined to belong to Mariah," Samantha added awkwardly. "And we're so grateful you gave it to her."

"But you're right, Auntie Hy," Mariah said serenely as she fingered the beautiful silver comb. "It *is* a California idea."

Craig laughed but Samantha felt flooded with nostalgia at

her daughter's innocent pride in her home state. Hyacinth moved on. "Well," she said, "I'm sure a Californian sensibility is very nice, but this second gift has a decidedly east coast flavor."

She delivered the yellow cube into Mariah's hands. "Oh, it's so heavy," Mariah said in surprise. She popped open the lid to be greeted with more tissue paper. She removed a large item and carefully unwrapped it. It was a crystal apple, engraved with the skyline of New York City. "How sweet," Mariah exclaimed. "The Big Apple!"

Hyacinth laughed. "Admittedly, this is the most whimsical of the three items. A charming little bauble my mother purchased decades ago when she was in the city. You can tell its age-" She softly touched a tiny piece of the skyline. "Notice the twin towers here. Clearly this was sculpted before the tragic events of September 11, 2001."

"I love it, Auntie Hy. Thank you so much!" She passed the apple to Samantha. "Careful, it's so heavy. But look at the little buildings. So beautiful."

Samantha took the apple in her hands then lifted it up to Craig. "Be good," she warned him, suspecting from his mischievous smirk that he was ready to play the holy fool. He didn't disappoint.

"Whoa," he said, balancing the apple in his palm. "Perfect size for a baseball! Mariah—you ready to bat?"

Mariah allowed herself her first giggle since her father's death. "Oh, stop!" she protested, planting a hand over her mouth.

"Yes, stop," Hyacinth said humorlessly.

Samantha leapt in, retrieving the apple and giving Craig a futile teacher-glare for his lack of remorse. "It truly was kind of you to take the trouble to bring these gifts on such short notice, Hyacinth."

"Oh, and I've saved the best for last," Hyacinth intoned, picking up the small jewel box. "I hope you will treasure this, Mariah, as so many women in our family have."

Mariah took a deep breath, looking so excited she was blinking back tears. With thumb and forefinger she lifted the lid and pulled out the obligatory tissue paper. Slowly unwrapping it, she found a gold thimble, engraved with the image of two hawks in profile, tail-to-tail and beak-to-beak, their wings spreading. Mariah gasped. "I've never seen anything like this!" she said in hushed surprise. "It's amazing! Mom, look--there's my hawk! My hawk and its twin have been engraved on this tiny gold thimble!"

"My goodness," Samantha said breathlessly. "They *are* hawks."

"Oh, no mere hawks!" Hyacinth said. "They're eagles. The Easters are a very patriotic family. The eagles are engraved on this thimble to symbolize our great love for this nation!"

"Oh, I'm sure we do love America," Mariah said nodding vigorously. "But Auntie Hy, this isn't an eagle--it's a red-tail or maybe a red-shouldered hawk. You can tell because the wings are so wide and rounded. A bald eagle's wings are somewhat narrow and plank-like. Plus the tail of this hawk on the thimble is shorter than an eagle's and the bill is less prominent."

"Oh, Mariah, Mariah!" Hyacinth interjected. "That's all very interesting, but there is no doubt that these are eagles on the thimble. My mother told me that, and my grandmother told me as well. Perhaps it doesn't meet all the criteria of bird lore you list, but they most certainly are intended to represent the great symbol of the United States of America. And that would be an eagle."

Samantha rose, ostensibly to get a better look. "She's right, Mariah," she said quickly, setting a conciliatory tone she hoped her daughter would emulate. "They're eagles."

Mariah caught the cue. "And I love it," she said quietly. "It means so much to me."

Hyacinth seated herself at the table. "As well it should, Mariah. This thimble has been in our family for generations. It's at least 150 years old."

"Wow!" Mariah exclaimed. "Where did it come from?"

"Well," Hyacinth mused, stretching out the word. "The story has been a bit obscured over the years, but it has been handed down from mother to daughter, and aunt to niece for many decades. I was told it was forged and engraved by a gold smith in Boston."

When Mariah passed the thimble to Samantha and Craig, Hyacinth warned that the trinket should be handled as little as possible. "Gold is a very soft metal," she informed them. "You wouldn't want to scratch it, or wear down the engraving. I always displayed it in a glass enclosed cabinet."

Tiring of Hyacinth in instructional mode, Samantha jumped in to offer refreshments. Hyacinth declined, saying she needed a nap before dinner. Mariah offered to make lemonade for Craig. He and Samantha headed outside to finish the yard work.

"Hawks," he said simply as they passed through the door.

"Right," Samantha said, relieved. "I guess that's what your vision was about. You weren't seeing a real hawk; it was the hawks on the thimble you were seeing."

"What makes you think the hawks on the Easter family thimble aren't real?" he asked. She rolled her eyes, but he seemed undeterred. "There's more to come, Samantha."

She sighed. "So you're playing the prophet for me this afternoon?"

"I'm not a prophet," he said as usual. "I just see what's

there for anyone to see."

"Right," Samantha retorted. "Anyone can see what you see. But don't you get that the rest of us don't know where to look?"

He had laughed his hearty laugh. "You know what I say is true, Samantha. There's more to come."

***

The limo pulled into the church lot as Samantha caught herself smiling, remembering Craig's exaggerated proclamation. She quickly bit her lip. Mariah was too young, she thought, too delicate, to adopt a ferocious predator as her totem. And Samantha was not ready to let her go. She reached over to grasp her daughter's hand.

Charlie had had broad shoulders and muscular legs from cycling and gardening and mowing the lawn. He was substantial and heavy and real in his hiking boots and khaki pants. He shaved every morning, but his beard was dark and grew quickly. At breakfast his cheeks would be pink but by noon his jaw was shadowed and in the evening his cheeks were stubbly and rough. Samantha thought when she had a baby with him that her daughter would be heavy like the earth; she didn't think she would be flighty with small feet and hands like she herself had. Samantha looked at her daughter and worried at Mariah's wan appearance. She seemed as thin as a piece of string. Samantha wanted to tie Mariah to her wrist so she wouldn't float away.

Getting out of the limo, Samantha was immediately surrounded by people--some she knew well, some not so well-- all wanting to pump her hand, to squeeze her shoulder, to murmur words of sympathy and encouragement. A few dared to press business cards into her palm, offering professional services of some sort. Samantha looked beyond them to a sky bruised with purple longing. She wished she could take Mariah and disappear somewhere--and perhaps this was not such an unrealistic wish. For that morning when Samantha awoke before dawn, unable to get back to sleep, she had remembered a secret she'd kept from her husband for nearly two decades. She called Craig, ready to ask for absolution. "I'm a millionaire," she whispered sadly.

"What are you talking about?" Craig asked.

"I never wanted this to happen. I feel so guilty."

"Again, I've got to ask--"

"He was such a dare devil. I knew if he left me a single mother, I'd need help."

"Samantha?"

"I bought a life insurance policy, years ago, before Mariah was even born. I paid the premium every month; I never even told him."

Craig laughed. "It was a good thing you did, Samantha. Don't feel guilty. Charlie approves. I can hear him cheering you on right now."

Samantha knew better than to ask Craig to come to the funeral. She knew his sensitivity to the thoughts and emotions of others had led him to adopt a hermit-like existence. "I'll be in your heart today," he said in conclusion. "You'll feel me there."

***

Samantha's gaze darted about, looking for Charlie's son Dale. She was worried about him. She was used to seeing him with his hair messed up, with dirt on his boots and grass stains on his khakis. He was not as gregarious as his father, but when he was with Charlie he was often loud and laughing. This week he had been so quiet. Well, that was to be expected. But Samantha had never seen him look so neat and clean. He worked as a lawyer, a well-paid corporate lawyer. He spent the bulk of his days in a business suit affecting a modulated business demeanor. The thought scared her. After all, *she* wasn't going to go out and play tackle football with him the way Charlie had. Would she never see her scruffy stepson again?

She was surprised to find herself craving a cigarette. She hadn't smoked a cigarette in well over forty years, not since she was in a crowded dorm room drinking Jack Daniels from a paper cup. She remembered herself wearing a pink dress and a necklace of red coral. She didn't know Charlie then. There were men before him, and there were men after him, but then one day the universe returned him to her and she was grateful. Today she would bury him and she didn't know what she would do after that.

Chapter Three

The placid lawn of the Catholic cemetery stretched for miles from the northern entrance—the domains of Saints Peter and Elizabeth—out to the sunny southern expanse presided over by Our Lady of Guadalupe. The coppery sheen of grave markers reflected midday sunshine, giving the impression that the gently rolling landscape had been secured by rows and rows of brass buttons. Potted chrysanthemums appeared randomly, adding pops of color as sharp as cheddar and mustard. The simple flowers, so hardy and familiar, had a grassy scent, not at all sweet, almost fetid. They served as a touchstone to the mundane, a reminder of the ordinariness of this ancient practice of returning to the dirt. In contrast, Mylar balloons, plastic Easter eggs, Styrofoam bunnies, and sagging silk daffodils lent an air of false festivity, a feeling that more than one person was trying too hard to gloss over the actuality of this place.

All we need is a hole in the ground, Dale thought wearily as he watched the undertakers arrange the stage with sprays of carnations and gladiolas on four-foot pedestals. Silver banners touting Charlie's status as "Beloved Husband & Father" and "Dearest Brother" were draped awkwardly between casket and flowers.

Dale had begged off riding in the limo, deferring to a half dozen of Samantha's cousins and her very elderly aunt. Thus he had appeared quite gallant, and his own Aunt Hy made a fuss over him, gushing that his unselfish gesture proved he was

37

a true Easter. She concluded by proclaiming he had "the Easter good looks and chiseled profile." That was a first. Most everyone had always said he looked like his Native American mother with his high cheekbones, narrow nose, and autumnal coloring. No matter. The truth was he wanted to ride alone to the service and cemetery in his van. He needed some time to himself between the foreign ritual of the church and the bustle that would surely accompany the reception. He didn't need this kind of a day to say good-by to his father. He'd rather have gone hiking or kayaking--that would have been a more fitting way for him to process this sudden loss, but he didn't want to let Samantha and Mariah down.

His father had pulled him aside one afternoon just a few weeks earlier to ramble on about "what if" scenarios. Charlie had been indirect—perhaps afraid to jinx himself by mentioning Death by name—but his meaning had been clear. Dale wondered now if Charlie had had some health concern that prompted the conversation. Maybe Dale should have urged his dad to see a doctor, but the thought hadn't even occurred him. Instead Dale had turned to talk about wills, trusts, insurance policies—the way he would have done with a client. He was sorry now, feeling he had somehow missed the point. Nonetheless, it had been easy for him to promise to look out for Samantha and Mariah. That was all Charlie seemed to care about.

So he had arrived promptly at the church to escort his stepmother and little sister down the center aisle behind his father's coffin. He had followed Sam's lead, standing and kneeling when appropriate. Outside the church he had skillfully deflected any overenthusiastic mourners who seemed to be taxing Samantha's energy.

But now, at the cemetery, he felt free to hang at the back of the group, behind the chairs, rocking back and forth on the balls of his feet. He thought about the pack of cigarettes hidden in his jacket pocket. He'd smoked as a teenager--much to his parents' dismay--but after milking that habit for all the parental hand wringing attention he felt he could muster, he'd given up the smokes in his early twenties. After his wife Jeannette had left him a scant nine months ago, he suddenly started thinking about smoking again. He'd been able to resist the urge. But on Sunday night, after learning of his father's death, he was in a mini mart filling up the van, and when he went in to pay, he'd picked up the pack of Camels. It was like a reflex. He'd only smoked five of them so far: five in five days, that wasn't so bad. He really wanted one right now. But Samantha and Mariah would smell it on him and give him hell, so he would have to let it go.

He didn't care that Jeannette wasn't there. The divorce was final two months ago, and he hadn't even called her. But truth be told, he wished his mother had flown out for the funeral. He knew it made no sense: why would she come? Geneva had had as little as possible to do with Charlie for nearly 30 years--ever since they'd split when Dale was barely in kindergarten. They'd never even been married. Dale knew he was the child of two young incautious lovers who miscalculated the need for a condom one night. He knew his parents loved him, but still there had been a time when he had envied baby Mariah's situation--born of a passionate but mature couple who accepted the responsibility of parenting better than Charlie and Dale's mother had. Over the years, his envy had given way to gratitude for his sister. He was happy to have both Mariah and Samantha in his life. But on this day, he missed his own mother.

Geneva was a statuesque Navajo woman who'd grown up on the reservation in Arizona. She was brilliant in math and history and had earned a scholarship to Dartmouth where she'd met and fallen for the young and clever Charlie Easter. Charlie was brilliant too, but growing up in privilege he didn't have Geneva's hunger. He was happy to hitch his wagon to hers and followed her to Berkeley, where he'd gotten an elementary teaching job while she sailed through law school at Bolt Hall. When she got pregnant, he resigned himself to a

California life, far away from the east coast he thought he loved.

But Geneva was content to build a life apart from the lover whom she considered a closed chapter of her youth. She gained minor fame as a Native American activist and defense attorney, finally accepting a position on the faculty at McGeorge. She married a superior court judge and the two lived in a mansion filled with original art on a hill overlooking the American River. They were quite the power couple in those days. But when Dale graduated high school, they sold the house and the cars, the sculpture and paintings, and moved back to Arizona where Geneva could work to help the poor there.

Dale had to admire that, but it was not the life for him. He was a native Californian, and he tired of both his parents whining about missing their childhood homes. Sure, he could understand why Geneva hadn't felt a need to come to Charlie's funeral, but he still wished that she had come out. For him. For her son.

The graveside service was beginning, and Aunt Hy came rushing to the back of the crowd. She did not approach Dale, but walked beyond the assemblage to turn and survey the long sweep of the cemetery's back lawn. She reminded Dale of a Dresden figurine that he'd seen perched on her mantle the summer twenty-some years ago when Charlie had taken his adolescent son back east to visit family stomping grounds. This tiny little statue depicted a woman with long arms and neck, pink cheeks and an upturned nose. "It's Aunt Hyacinth, isn't it?" he had asked his grandmother.

"Don't be silly," she replied. "It's an antique."

He didn't understand. It was porcelain and perfect. That was Aunt Hy in a nutshell.

As he glanced back at her half turned profile, he heard her sharp intake of breath. Her chin was quivering and a low gurgling sound was erupting from her throat. He was stunned to see this crack in her tidy exterior, but perhaps Hyacinth was more upset than he had realized at leaving her brother to be buried way out here in California. A swell of sympathy for her rose in his solar plexus and he had to swallow hard to tamp down a sudden urge to tear up and sob with her. So here was another Easter tradition, suitable for both aunt and nephew: a manly squelching of emotion. That wasn't his dad's style, but now he knew his own habit had a family precedent.

A hummingbird zipped by him, the loud whir of its frantic wings jolting him out of his reverie. The bird was a burst of color, scarlet and green, blurring with the speed of an arrow. Without thought, Dale turned, watching it disappear in a play of sunlight. Just then he caught sight of another woman striding across the lawn. She was large with broad shoulders, dressed in sleek black pants, black blouse, and black scarf draped over her head. She advanced rapidly like a soldier, marching, marching. Dale blinked at the sight of her. She seemed adorned in glass or strips of silver, for sunlight seemed to bounce off her wrists and throat. As she came near, her scarf slipped to her shoulders, and her face and hair throbbed like a chunk of white quartz in the noon sun. Her skin was white, her slicked back hair was white, her lips were smeared with ruby lipstick making her mouth look distorted and bloody. She had sharp angular cheeks and jaw, a pointy nose and chin.

Dale squinted, curious to see if he could discern the color of her eyes. She was as pale as an albino and he expected that her eyes might be pink. She paused at the edge of the crowd, her head gliding from side to side. Dale started as his gaze met hers. Her eyes were as green as lime Jell-O.

She stared straight ahead now, unblinking as the priest raised his arms to sprinkle the casket with holy water. Suddenly her face crumpled, tears streamed down her pale cheeks and her chest heaved. She tipped back her head as if ready to howl—but all in eerie silence. Dale was mesmerized.

Who was this woman? She looked like she'd come straight out of a cheap horror movie.

***

Charlie had equated the midtown bungalow with his wife—an old fashioned notion to be sure, but one imbued with a deep romanticism. When he and Dale were out at the gym or stopped at *Fox and Goose* for beer and fries, Charlie would suddenly announce it was time to go. "Gotta get back to my sanctuary," he'd say, clapping Dale on the shoulder, and Dale knew his father was referring both to the house and to Samantha. He was never quite sure what Charlie meant by this, but Dale knew he didn't feel that way about Jeannette.

Charlie liked loud places and loud people: boisterous pick-up basketball games, night clubs with loud music, art gallery receptions with energetic students and argumentative intellectuals blasted on cheap red wine and bite-size cubes of cheese.

But the bungalow was always quiet. Music was soft, fruit was fresh and pastries were home-baked. It wasn't that Charlie was deferring to the ambience set by Samantha. No, Charlie considered his home a temple, and sometimes—not always, but often—Charlie liked to whisper.

Today the house was unfamiliar. Sitting at a card table next to his little sister, Dale could feel the floor reverberating with the frenetic laughter and shouts that characterized the YMCA gymnasium or the *Fox and Goose* on open mic night. Dale recognized a lot of these people from the gym and the bar. They were musicians and artists, aerobic instructors and evangelical choir members. They had heavy feet and deep voices. Mariah sat beside him picking at a plate filled with salads and chunks of cheese. She seemed undisturbed, but perhaps this was no louder than her school cafeteria. "Where's your mom?" he asked her, and Mariah turned toward the kitchen.

"Mom's hiding," she confided.

Dale caught sight of his stepmother standing in the archway between the kitchen and dining room, her neck twisted at a seemingly impossible angle as she watched the many people swirling around like moths. Samantha seemed tense, a dark vertical line descending between her deep eyes. "Maybe I should go help her," Dale said but Mariah tapped his sleeve.

"Wait, my boyfriend Todd has arrived. You should meet him."

Dale followed his sister's gaze to light on a tall young man who had just bellied up to the buffet table. Nice—the kid grabs a plate before greeting his girlfriend. *What a swell guy.*

"How come he didn't come to the church?" Dale asked, trying but failing to sound gentle.

Mariah stared at her fork as she pushed around out-of-season grapes and cantaloupe. "Well," she began, rolling her eyes, looking embarrassed. "He's decided he can't go to Christian services anymore. He's decided he's a pagan."

Dale took a quick gulp of beer. As a lawyer, he'd made a career out of affecting a cool, detached demeanor. But now he was angry.

He remembered a year or more ago, after beating his father in a one-on-one game of HORSE, they had sat on the bleachers at the Y, drinking canned soda, and Charlie had told him how proud he was. "Proud of both of us, really," he said. "Proud you've got that hunger to win. Proud of myself that I taught you it was okay to go for it." They sipped their colas and Charlie went on. "That boy Mariah's seeing—he's got no drive. I can beat him every time."

And maybe nobody's good enough for your little girl, Dale thought. "Maybe sports aren't his thing," Dale said, wanting to defend the poor kid, whoever he was.

"He's on the team," Charlie retorted. "First string on the school team."

"Oh." Then Dale laughed. "Well, old man, sounds like the kid is letting his girlfriend's father beat him. Tell him to take off the gloves. Let you see what he's made of."

"You think I haven't done that?" Charlie shook his head. "He'll never be able to keep up with Mariah. He just doesn't want it bad enough."

Dale looked at Todd now as the caterer heaped rare roast beef onto his plate. He was a good-looking kid, brown hair and blue eyes, solid forehead but a weak jaw.

"Todd told me," Mariah said suddenly, "that he was going to become a vegan. You know, now that he's a pagan." Dale tightened his grip on his bottle of Mexican beer.

Todd seated himself next to Mariah and Dale stared at him intensely. "Todd," Mariah said softly, "this is my brother Dale." Todd extended his hand, and Dale enveloped it in a tight grip. "You treating my little sister right?" he said bluntly. Mariah's mouth dropped open. "Dale--" she began, but Todd cut her off.

"It's okay, that's his right." He turned to Dale with a leering glint in his eye. "I can assure you, sir, I know how to satisfy her."

Dale saw Mariah rear back. It was all he could do to stay in his chair, but his sister grabbed his arm. "Let me speak, Dale," she cautioned. "Todd," she said, shifting gears without pause. "I'm glad you could come today, and enjoy this meal in memory of my father. Our father--Dale's and mine. But after this I can't keep seeing you. I'm breaking up with you."

Todd put down his sandwich. "Mariah," he said. "You've just had a big shock, honey, what with your father's death and all. I don't think you really want to do this. Let's give it a rest for a few days--" He stopped to shove a heaping forkful of pasta salad in his pie hole. "It'll all be okay, babe."

"No, Todd; it won't be okay," Mariah retorted. "You see, a few minutes ago I realized that I don't like you. I guess I never really did like you much, but you are very good looking. I'm sorry to have been so shallow, but you know, that kind of thing happens when you're seventeen."

Dale shifted quickly on the folding chair, nearly dropping his beer bottle. He wasn't sure if that was the most brilliant or least sensitive break-up line he'd ever heard. No matter. He knew his role: when one of his clients made a decision, it was his job to see it was executed. In this case he was happy to do the same for his sister. "Uh, Todd," Dale said in a low voice. "Can I get you a To Go bag?"

"Oh, that's not necessary, Dale," Mariah interjected. "He's welcome to stay and finish his meal. Let's give him some space." She rose abruptly. "Good-bye, Todd."

Dale followed her to another table on the other side of the room. "I hope I didn't force you into that in some way," Dale said though he wasn't the least bit sorry.

"I've known I should do that for a long time. I was ready now."

They sat silently watching the parade of people fluttering by. Hyacinth strode through the throngs, her silvery laughter tinkling first in one corner of the room, and then the other. "Be thankful your mom doesn't own a piano," Dale whispered. "Aunt Hy would be leading us all in show tunes and patriotic songs. I can still remember her singing 'It's a Grand Old Flag,' at Poppy's funeral back when I was 15."

Mariah's eyes widened. "No, she didn't. You're making that up."

"I kid you not."

"Oh, Dale--look!" Mariah pointed discreetly as a pale woman with slicked back hair dropped a crumpled cocktail napkin into Samantha's Chinese vase. "That's not a waste basket! That's so disrespectful."

"I saw that woman at the cemetery," Dale noted. "She was bawling her eyes out. Who is she?"

"I don't know," Mariah said indignantly. "But she shouldn't put garbage in my mother's vase."

"Relax, Mare. One little dirty napkin won't break the vase. It'll be okay."

"But Mom loves that vase."

He nodded. "I remember when Dad bought her that vase. Gosh, years ago. There was this Asian import store out in Rancho Cordova. He used to take me there some weekends-- said he liked the energy in there." Dale shook his head. "I never quite understood that energy stuff, but he liked this place. It was quiet, it was peaceful, and he had his eye on this vase for months. He wanted to buy it for your mom because she likes tigers."

"Yeah, I like the tigers on that vase. The two of them together; it's so sweet."

"I guess," Dale agreed with a shrug. "So he had it on lay away, paying it off twenty dollars a month or so. It was going to take him over a year at that rate! But he broke down and spent all his change on it when your mom had the miscarriage."

Dale saw his sister's back stiffen. "She had a miscarriage? When was that? Before I was born?"

"Well, yeah, it would have had to be, wouldn't it? I guess it wasn't actually a miscarriage. No, it was a tubal pregnancy. That's what it was--the fetus was lodged in one of her Fallopian tube so they had to remove it."

"I didn't know about that," Mariah said.

"You didn't?" Dale asked. "Hmm. I wonder why they never told you?"

"Well, I guess since it was before I was born--" Mariah mused.

"Right, it was before you were born," Dale continued, "because you made it through the tube--you know into the uterus--but your twin--your twin was stuck in the tube."

Mariah's hand flew up to her throat. "My twin? What are you talking about?"

Dale stared at her, feeling ill. "Maybe you should ask your mom."

"No, Dale, please tell me. I want to know."

He took another sip of his beer. "Well, if I'm remembering it right, this tubal pregnancy happened when she was pregnant with you. She was pregnant with twins, but only one of the fetuses--and that would be you!--made it into her uterus. The other fetus--your twin--was lodged in the tube."

Mariah balled up a bit of the tablecloth in her fist. "I had a twin?"

"Well, yeah, I guess so."

"Was it a boy or a girl?"

Dale bit his lip, full of regret. "I don't know, Mariah. I think it was too early to tell."

Mariah sat at the table stunned. "A twin," she repeated.

"I shouldn't have told you," Dale said. "I'm sorry. I upset you."

"Oh, no, Dale, I'm not upset. I'm--" she paused, waving her hand in a futile gesture. "I'm--amazed! I'm just amazed."

She leaned back in her chair. She didn't even seem to notice Hyacinth's husky singing voice leading the crowd in a medley of Beatles' songs.

Chapter Four

Samantha stood in the kitchen watching the flurry of activity around her as if she were an entomologist observing the behavior of swarming bees. Hyacinth was in the dining room singing *Surfer Girl,* having announced to the crowd that it was Charlie's favorite. Where the hell had she gotten an idea like that? Charlie hadn't even owned a Beach Boys album.

She peeked through the kitchen door to get a better look, and not for the first time, wondered whom all these people were who had shown up to mourn Charlie Easter. Unlike herself, Charlie was an extrovert. He collected people wherever he went--musicians, artists, ministers and aerobic instructors. Her own co-workers and cousins had already left, though a few close friends stood sentry with her in the kitchen overseeing the caterer's handling of the dishwasher and desserts. She wondered how she would ever get these people out of her house, and decided that maybe it didn't matter. She could neither beat 'em nor join 'em, but she could quietly retreat. She squeezed her way through the throng gathered around her sister-in-law and headed down the hallway to take refuge in her bedroom.

As she passed her office cum guest room Dale nearly ran into her as he surreptitiously slid through the door. He looked guilty, caught red-handed doing something he shouldn't, but Samantha was happy to see a friendly face. "You okay?" she asked.

"I'm fine," he said hastily.

She smiled. "You hiding out in here? You got a look about you like you're up to no good!"

He rolled his eyes. "I guess there no point in having a secret on a day like today," he confessed. "Come here." He ushered her into her own office. "You know, Sam, I don't think I'd ever been in this room before Monday when I brought Aunt Hy's luggage in here. It was your office. I had no need--and no invitation--to come in here over the years. But when I came in here the other day--" he paused to take a deep breath, "it's kind of silly, but I saw this photo." He gestured to a corner where Samantha had accumulated a wide collection of photos taken over many years and places: she and Charlie on their wedding day holding baby Mariah in a flower strewn basket between them; Dale holding Mariah on that same day, the day he was his dad's eighteen-year-old best man. There were some old black and whites of Samantha's parents, and a small photo of Charlie's mom and dad waving from the deck of a ship. Several unframed snapshots of Samantha's students adorned a cork bulletin board. "Here's the one I'm talking about," Dale told her, as he pointed to an eight by ten framed color shot of a beautiful dark haired woman with chocolate brown eyes and voluptuous lips. She seemed to have an amber glow emanating from her skin. He couldn't take his eyes off the photo. "Now if I were a man like my father--fond of romantic notions like destiny and spiritual quests--I'd say that when I saw this picture I fell in love at first sight, that I have seen the woman I am destined to love! But that's pretty silly." He started to get a little bleary eyed and Samantha threw her arms around his tall frame.

Dale accepted her embrace as he wiped at his eyes with his fingers. "I'm probably missing my dad so I decided to invent a story like he always did."

"Maybe," Samantha said.

"Anyway," Dale concluded, pulling back and coughing, "I had to come in here and take another look at this beautiful woman. I was hoping that a second look would convince me I was 'writing a story in my head,' as Dad would say."

"But she's still a fairy tale beauty, huh?" Samantha said. "No matter how many times you come back to convince yourself otherwise."

Dale shrugged. "So what's she like, Samantha? Is she single? Do you think I've got a chance with her? I sound like a high school kid." He threw up his hands, pretending he was joking. "Let's go have some coffee and dessert."

Samantha grabbed his hand. "That's Luisa—and she is the most courageous person I've ever known. She moved back east to Connecticut with her mother years ago, right after she was in my class. But she loves to correspond with people on the internet. I think she would be open to an email relationship--and I think it would do you good right now to talk to her online. She's young but very wise."

"Well, if she lives 3,000 miles away, I guess the internet would be the way to go these days."

Samantha continued to hold Dale's hand. "I don't know that you could ever have anything more than that with her, Dale. You see, Luisa is severely autistic."

"Autistic---those are the kids you work with, right?"

"Some of them are, but not all," Samantha sighed, unsure if she had the energy for all the thoughts swirling in her head right now. "They call it a spectrum disorder now--because people with autism can have so many varying degrees. Some people are extremely intelligent, geniuses even; others have severe intellectual disabilities. Some pass easily for neuro-typical, though they might seem a little quirky or compulsive, obsessed with things like science fiction fantasies or trains. Others appear to be very disabled, unable to control their bodies or speak." She paused, taking a deep breath. "Dale, Luisa is non verbal; she has never learned to speak. She sometimes has trouble controlling her movements, she rocks back and forth to sooth herself, and sometimes she stims—or stimulates herself—on moving objects like the blades of a fan or on her own waving fingers. But she is extremely intelligent and she's learned to communicate through typing. She is brave and amazing, Dale. I would love for you to meet her."

Dale stared at Samantha, his mouth open, his fingers twitching. Samantha was sure she had disappointed and perhaps even overwhelmed him with her description of Luisa's symptoms. "Well," she said, giving his hand a final squeeze, "you think about it, and--"

"I don't need to think about it," he said, grasping her hand tighter. "I would love to meet Luisa."

***

Mariah stood in her parents' bedroom, holding the golden thimble, fingering the sharp grooves of the engraved hawks. She felt bad she had been impolite to Aunt Hyacinth, but there was no doubt that these birds were red-tailed hawks, not eagles. She wondered if the goldsmith had had a particular affinity for the red-tail over an eagle, or if he had made some kind of a mistake. She opened her palm and looked carefully at each little line etched into the sides. She could hear her father's voice: no coincidences, no mistakes! In other words, even if the goldsmith had intended to carve an eagle all those decades ago, he hadn't--he'd carved a red-tail, and she should trust that message.

The conversation she had just had with Dale had been disturbing and exciting at the same time. She had had a twin! What a miraculous discovery. Somehow it made her feel more special and yet more lonely. She'd always felt that something was missing in her life, but she was never quite sure what it was. When her friends started pairing up with boys, she'd done the same so she could fit in. She thought it would fill this great hollow place inside of her, but she'd been wrong. Being with Todd had made her feel more hollow, more alone. She thought of the afternoons she'd spent in the gym, perched on the bleachers watching him play intramural basketball, of the evenings she'd spent with him at parties, slow dancing, his hands moving up and down her back: how boring it had all been. How unmoved she felt when he touched her or kissed her. Still she managed to put on a happy front, to giggle with the other girls, to play the demure ingénue when they were out with other couples. And that was why she'd done it, wasn't it? So she could continue to be one of the crowd, going bowling or playing laser tag, double dating at a movie or dinner at the pizza parlor--that was the most fun--to be with everyone. So she had to hold Todd's hand, sit on his lap, and dance all night with him instead of taking turns the way they all used to do. He was the best-looking boy, and though it made her feel shallow, she was proud he chose her. But still, she had to admit it, she was bored.

She didn't mean to blame him, she realized now that it didn't have anything to do with him. She had felt incomplete-- and isn't that how a woman completes herself?--with a man? Oh, her mother always said that wasn't true, and even her father had said that she could be anything she wanted to be-- but everywhere you looked folks were coupled up--and you couldn't go to the special dances like junior prom or senior ball without a date. You just couldn't. So when Todd asked her to wear his ring, she said, sure, why not? He was no better or worse than any of the other boys available to her. Why shouldn't she hang out with him? And when he wanted her to go all the way, she thought--well, it's got to be somebody, why not him? It seemed a practical decision because they say it can hurt the first time, and Todd was pretty small down there. She made him wear a condom and it all worked out fine.

She wondered if she'd had her twin--a brother or a sister who was the same age and size as she was--she wondered if she would have felt a need to try to fit in with everybody else. There was really no way to know. But somehow this thimble made her feel more sure of herself, more complete within herself. She didn't know why. She knew it didn't make any sense. Maybe knowing she was part of a larger legacy had had an effect on her. Or maybe it was the idea playing at the edge of her awareness, this silly thought that she didn't even dare form all the way: could it be that her twin--the entity who was supposed to have been her twin--might that person have been born somewhere else? Maybe this person was looking for her too? She looked at the twin birds engraved in gold. Maybe the entity hadn't incarnated in human form. Maybe she was a hawk.

Samantha opened the door and disturbed Mariah's reverie. "Oh, Mariah," her mother exclaimed, "I was wondering where you were! Are you okay?'

"I needed a breather," she said.

"You and I had the same idea," Samantha admitted as she sank down on Charlie's side of the bed. Mariah carefully placed the thimble in its box on the nightstand near the bathroom, then climbed over the bed to sit on her mother's usual side. They leaned back against the headboard, their legs stretched out before them, and automatically they held hands. Samantha sighed with fatigue.

"Mom," Mariah said slowly. "Dale told me that before I was born--um, that you had a tubal pregnancy--that I had a twin who died before birth."

"He told you that?" Samantha said sadly. "Why would he tell you that today I wonder?"

"He didn't mean any harm, Mom," Mariah said quickly. "He thought I knew. And I guess I'm wondering why I didn't know, why you and Daddy never told me?"

Samantha sighed. "I don't know, baby. To be honest, I

don't think about it much anymore. It was very upsetting at the time. But then I had you! And nothing could have made me happier!"

"Dale told me Daddy bought you the big ginger jar vase when you had to have surgery, when you had the tubal pregnancy."

"Oh," Samantha said, looking thoughtful. "No, that's not exactly true. He did give me the vase when he found out I was pregnant with you, but--" She paused and shook her head. "You know, it's kind of a complicated story, Mariah. Maybe we should save it for another day."

"Mom! I want to know."

Mariah watched her mother sigh and could hear the exhaustion in her voice. "Okay," Samantha said.

Mariah knew she should acquiesce and allow her mother to postpone the telling, but her eagerness to know the truth was thumping in her solar plexus, threatening to escape from her throat. She chewed on the corner of her mouth, willing herself to stay quiet. "This is what happened," Samantha began. "You remember I told you your dad and I met when we were both--well, not really young, in our late 20s. Then we broke up and later we ran into each other again, and we decided to--um, you know, we were dating again."

"You mean you were sleeping together?" Mariah asked bluntly.

Samantha cocked an eyebrow at Mariah. "Well that is how pregnancy happens. But if you want the details--well, I'm not going to tell you every detail, but I will say this--we had spent one night together and then he disappeared. Just like that, he was gone. And to be honest I wasn't all that surprised. Your dad could be like that back then."

"Are all men like that?"

"Oh, no, Mariah, not all of them. And your dad didn't mean to be that way--well, I mean, it turned out that he'd left town suddenly because Hyacinth had called him to say that their mom had had a stroke. So he'd jumped on a plane and went back to Connecticut and he was so worried about your grandmother that he didn't think he needed to call me. But see he didn't know I was pregnant."

"Oh, well," Mariah said hopefully, "he wouldn't have disappeared if he'd known you were pregnant, would he?"

"Well, he didn't disappear once he did find out, did he?" Samantha pointed out. "But you see--I wanted to be sure he loved me--you know, for myself--not just because I was pregnant, so when he finally did call me from back east, I didn't tell him about the pregnancy. And I didn't tell him that I'd had to have surgery because of a tubal pregnancy. I kept all that from him. So he didn't know. But then one day he called me and he said he wanted to be with me here in California--so he'd come home to me! And he said, Sam, can I come see you now? And I said, yes, of course! And he said, good, because I'm on your front porch. And I looked out and there he was! I knew that as soon as I opened the door he would see that I was pregnant. But I knew it would be okay, because he was choosing to be with me even if I wasn't pregnant."

Samantha smiled and nodded at her daughter but Mariah still felt anxious. "But what if he didn't want to have a baby? Weren't you scared that maybe he wouldn't want *me?*"

Samantha nodded. "Yes, I guess I was a little scared. But I knew Charlie had always been a good father to Dale--so I felt pretty hopeful that when I opened the door he'd be happy to see both you and me!" Her tears were flowing down her cheeks now. "And I was right. When he saw my condition, he got down on his knees and put his ear up to my belly button, and he said, 'Sam I love you, and I hope this baby is mine, but even if it's not, I want to be here with you and the baby.' And I said, 'Of course she's yours. She's your daughter.' And he came inside, and that was that. We were together every night after that."

Mariah rested her head on her mother's shoulder. "Oh, that's the best story ever, Mom," she said. "But, you know, I still wish I'd had a twin."

Samantha drew back to look at her daughter's face. "I'm sorry, Mariah," she said, still allowing her tears to stream freely. "Have you always been lonely? Or is it just today--now that your dad is gone?"

"Oh, Mommy, don't worry about me, this is the way it's supposed to be for me I guess." She paused to clear her throat. "It's not so much a loneliness, it's a feeling of incompleteness. I've always felt this way, and now I know why."

"But baby," Samantha pleaded, "a lot of young people feel that. It's a function of youth, of feeling confused about where you're going to go and what you're going to do. It really does get better when you're older."

Mariah stared down at her hands, knowing she had disturbed her mother with this stubborn pessimism. "Maybe," she said, trying to rein in her emotion. "It'll be okay. I'm sure you're right."

Samantha looked at her, her mouth open and her eyebrows raised. Now Mariah felt bad and resolved to change the subject. "Mom," she said with feigned brightness, "do you think my twin is out there somewhere?"

Samantha lowered her chin, seeming surprised at this new question to ponder. "I don't know. Do you mean like a soul mate?"

"No," Mariah said insistently. "I mean my twin--my actual twin. I mean the entity that had at first intended to incarnate as my twin, through you and Daddy, but instead didn't make it into your uterus. Do you think that entity went into another womb and was born somewhere else?"

Samantha smiled. "I think that's a good question for Craig. As for me, your guess is as good as mine."

"You know what I think?" Mariah asked.

"No--what?"

"I think my twin became a hawk. That's why the hawk came to me--and that's why the Easter family thimble has two hawks on it."

Samantha laughed. "I'm thinking a story like this would give Aunt Hy nightmares! But I like it and what's more--" A sound in the adjoining bathroom stopped her comment. "What was that?"

Mariah leaned forward to look past her mother. "I don't know. Sounded like a bottle hitting the floor."

The sound of shattering glass exploded in their ears. The pale woman burst out of the tiny bathroom, screeching and lifting her hands in a shocking display of attack readiness. Her hair was no longer swept back but flew wildly from her scalp like white kelp, her mouth looked bloodied with ruby lipstick and her nose was sharp as a fish hook. Samantha leapt to her feet. She set her face mere inches from the woman's contorted countenance. "Who the fuck are you and what the hell are you doing in my bedroom?"

Mariah gasped at her mother's coarse language, but she was proud of her too. Her mother was as patient as they come; she was a special education teacher, for goodness sake! But on today of all days, she shouldn't have to be patient and helpful. How dare this strange looking woman hide in Mom's bathroom! She was eavesdropping on a private conversation! A line had been crossed.

"Get the fuck out of my bedroom and out of my house!"

Samantha shouted. She lifted her arm and pointed to the door.

But Pale-Woman only screeched again like some large ugly bird. This ghoulish crone lifted her skinny arms suddenly, pushing her claw-like hands onto Samantha's chest and stomach, roughly shoving her back onto the bed. In one swift motion she grabbed the boxed thimble off the nightstand and leapt toward the bathroom door.

"Mom!" Mariah yelled. "She's got my thimble!"

At that, Samantha jumped up and threw herself on the retreating woman's back. They fell to the floor, Samantha on top. "Drop it! You drop it now!" Samantha screamed. But Pale-Woman lifted herself up off the floor, even with Samantha still clinging to her black jacket. She shook Samantha off as if Samantha were a kitten. Lifting both hands above her head she took off like a Marvel comics character, crashing through the window, glass shards scattering. Samantha lifted herself onto her elbows and gaped. Perhaps Pale-Woman had jumped out the window, but it sure as heck looked like she had flown.

Mariah threw herself down beside her mother. "Are you all right? Can you stand?"

"Yes, it's okay, Mariah, I'm okay," Samantha mumbled, but Mariah could see her mother was holding her head bowed at an odd angle. She looked weak and dizzy. Mariah clung to her protectively, as if she had experienced another death, another violation.

Dale burst in from the hallway. "What's going on?" he exclaimed. "Are you both all right?"

"My thimble!" Mariah cried. "That awful pale woman, Dale--you remember we saw her throw trash in Mom's vase--that awful crazy woman--she stole my thimble!"

By now, Hyacinth was pushing her way into the room at Dale's elbow. "Someone's stolen the Easter family thimble?

That's outrageous! Call the police at once."

Dale looked to Samantha to be a calming voice. "Samantha?" he asked, as he helped her to her feet. "What do you want to do?"

Samantha's hands and chin were trembling, but Mariah couldn't tell if her mother shook with weakness or anger. Samantha looked up at Dale and her eyes grew wide. "Damn right we're calling the police," she declared. "That woman attacked my daughter and me on the day of my husband's funeral--" Her voice cracked then. She swallowed hard as tears streamed down her cheeks.

Dale pulled her into his arms. "Shh--I'll take care of it. You and Mariah rest. I'll call 911."

He left her side to pick up the phone. Hyacinth sidled up to her. "What can I get you, sweetheart?" Hyacinth asked. "Tea or whiskey?"

Samantha nodded. "You know what, Hy? I think I'll have a little of both."

***

Dale perched glumly in the dining room, feeling that he had somehow let his father down. Mariah was pacing futilely through the house and yard, searching for some sign of her thimble and the strange women who had taken it. Samantha and Hyacinth were sitting cozily on the couch, each cradling a cup of spiked tea. "He loved Beach Boy songs when we were growing up." Dale heard Hyacinth say. "He talked about coming out west for years. He was dying to see the Pacific Ocean."

"Why, that rat bastard!" Samantha squealed in an uncharacteristic falsetto. "Telling me all the time how he was home sick for the woods of New England. He'd listen to James Taylor for hours, singing about the Berkshires and the road

60

from Stockbridge to Boston." Soon they were weeping, then giggling, then harmonizing lines from *California Girls.*

Mariah darted back in, asking if the police had come. "Not yet," Dale told her.

"What's taking them so long?" she demanded. Dale considered telling her that theft was not as high a priority as some other crimes, say assault or rape, but he didn't think it wise to go there. "How bout we watch some TV or pop in a DVD while we're waiting?" he suggested.

"Not now," Mariah said in a clipped tone as she strode out the front door. Dale sighed. At least the theft had served to clear the mourners from the house. No one was left except for the caterers who were boxing leftovers and washing dishes in the kitchen.

When an officer finally arrived Dale escorted him in to take his stepmother's statement. "Oh, officer," Samantha said. "You don't need to worry about me. But you must speak to my daughter. That woman stole something very important to her. Yes, I know it sounds silly, but it was no ordinary thimble! You go online, you'll see, there are lots of very valuable thimbles on the market, antiques, collectables. They're like little family crests, little badges of honor. You can find them engraved with tiny animals on them, or miniature maps of European countries, state flowers and birds. It's quite remarkable. My mother used to have one with a little Hummel child painted on it. Of course it wasn't very practical; it was just for show. She never used it to sew with. Don't know whatever happened to it, I suppose we sold it at the estate sale. Oh, yes, thank you, Hyacinth, I will have more tea. Where's Mariah, Dale? She needs to speak with the police officer."

Dale took Samantha's cup from his aunt. "She's not used to such strong 'tea,' Hyacinth," he cautioned. "Let's ease up a little, okay?"

"Yoursh father would besh sho proud of yous Dale,"

Hyacinth slurred, and Dale nearly dropped the teacup. Everything had been so ordered and controlled; now it was splitting at the seams. Where was Mariah?

"Sir," the officer pulled Dale aside. "My sympathies at your loss, but I have to ask if you can tell me what really happened here. This story sounds rather fantastic. Considering your mother's lack of sobriety--"

"Hey," Dale blurted out, "this is completely legit! I didn't see the attack, but Samantha--my stepmother--was completely sober when it happened. The attacker was here. I saw her myself! In fact I saw her at the cemetery too. She came striding across the lawn--she was tall and striking--stark white skin and white hair, deep red lipstick--she looked alien, like something out of a horror movie, very creepy. She stood at the back of the crowd and cried like crazy! Tears flooded down her cheeks and her whole body was heaving. It was outrageous! Nobody knew who she was. That was the weird thing--who was she? Bawling her eyes out over my father's grave, when nobody knew her? Did she really know my father or was she some kind of funeral geek haunting the bereaved, taking advantage of their hospitality and their vulnerability?"

Dale was on a roll now; but the officer interrupted him. "So white skin, white hair, red lips--did it look like her skin was naturally pale or was she wearing make-up?"

Dale stared at the man. "I don't know."

Mariah came rushing through the front door then, breathless and wet eyed. "Did you find her?" she cried at once, accosting the officer, nearly grabbing the pencil from his hand. "Did you tell him what she looked like, Dale? Did you tell him how she threw that napkin in my mother's vase? That's important, you know. Did you tell him?"

Dale sighed. "Mariah, it's disgusting, but it's not illegal to be so gauche," he pointed out.

"But Dale!" she said insistently. "Dale, listen! Officer, this awful woman who attacked my mother--she threw a napkin into my mother's vase. That vase over there!" She crossed the room and reached into the large ginger jar. "Wait'll you see this!"

"Miss--" the officer began to admonish her, but Mariah seemed not to hear him.

"It's still in here!" She grinned triumphantly. "Don't you see? It will have her DNA on it! You'll be able to get her DNA from this napkin and then you'll find out who she is, and then you'll find my thimble!"

The officer glanced over at Dale and Dale knew the man was hoping he understood. He did understand; he didn't want to be the one who understood, but he did. "Mariah, sweetie-- that stuff only works on TV shows. I don't think they'll be able to do that."

"Why not? I don't see why not! This is important!"

The officer nodded slowly, "Your uncle is right, miss," he began, but again he was interrupted.

"He's my brother," Mariah yelled, her voice cracking. "Dale is my brother and our father died this week and we buried him today, and we can't have this happen! I need you to get my thimble back!"

Then Samantha, looking very steady, was at her daughter's side, embracing her and pressing Mariah's face against her chest as if her daughter were a small child who had skinned a knee or elbow. She nodded to the officer. "You're probably used to seeing people fall apart, huh? I mean it happens all the time in your job."

"Yes, Ma'am," the officer said slowly. "I'm sorry I can't help you with what's really upsetting you all, but I'll take down the information, get you a report number for your insurance agent."

"What do you mean a report for the insurance?" Mariah demanded.

Samantha brushed the hair away from Mariah's face. "Baby," she said, "I think the thimble is gone."

"No!" Mariah squealed.

"Come sit with me, babe," Samantha soothed.

"But, Mom--"

"Dale will talk to the officer--"

"Of course," Dale jumped in, finally feeling useful again as he led the man toward the kitchen.

"No, Mom! Officer! We've got to find it! It's my legacy! The Easter family legacy!"

"Now, Miss," the officer said optimistically, "we'll definitely be looking for this woman. She sounds dangerous and she may be preying on more folks like you who have suffered a loss. Maybe we'll even find your trinket. I don't know, it's possible."

"But you have to!"

"You know, Miss," he continued, "you might try going to pawn shops or even looking on e-bay, places like that. That's what people do now-a-days--they don't need fences, they go selling the stolen goods online. You might check that."

"Sure, Mariah," Dale assured her. "I'll help with that. We'll find something."

"Something? We can't just find *some*thing! We need to find *my* thimble. How could someone take something that so clearly belonged with me? I don't understand."

Chapter Five

The next day Dale stood on the balcony of his new condo overlooking Capitol Park, smoking a cigarette. He'd made it through the funeral and the crazy reception and hadn't smoked a single one. But today this was his second and it wasn't even noon.

His ex-wife Jeannette had called before nine. "I wanted to say how sorry I was about your dad," she said. "I saw the obituary in the paper, but you didn't call, so I thought I better stay away."

"You could've come if you'd wanted to," he said lamely. He held his breath, knowing he was lying. He was relieved she hadn't put in an appearance.

He had met her at a legal conference at the Hyatt six years ago. She was an event planner for the hotel and she'd organized the conference for the bar association. The "event planner" title didn't do her justice: she supervised over a hundred employees at that time. Within two years she was coordinating activities at hotels up and down the west coast. Dale had never met anyone more extroverted, more organized, or more extravagant. He even teased her once that she had too many letters in her name. That hadn't set well.

She cleared her throat. "Dale, you know, we didn't part on the best of terms and I--well, it was a time for you to be with your family. I didn't want to intrude."

"Hey, you're family," Dale said automatically. "I'm sure Samantha and Mariah would have been happy to see you." Now that was true. The women of the family would have welcomed Jeannette. Dale, himself—well, not so much.

"Okay," she said tartly. "My fault. I'm sorry; I should have come."

"I didn't say that. Jeez, Jen, don't make a big deal about this. I appreciate you wanted to do the right thing." He sighed. He knew it was just as much his fault as hers, but somehow conversation with Jen always seemed to take this bitter turn.

Back when they were first dating, just being with Jeannette gave Dale a rush like skiing or skateboarding. She was intelligent and funny: he had to work to keep up with her and he liked that. They were good together. They latched onto a party and charity event circuit that enhanced both their careers. They were able to introduce each other to the right people.

When they got married, they bought a Craftsman mansion in east Sacramento and Jeannette went right to work rehabbing it. She had a lot of contacts and was able to trade favors for bargain prices. She made that house and yard into a showcase: it looked like it had been staged for market.

Dale had been proud of Jeannette for how hard she'd worked on the project. But one evening he returned early, before his wife, and there, alone in his own living room, he felt as if he was walking into an unfamiliar B&B. The place wasn't his home. It was something you'd see in a Pottery Barn catalog.

"You need to spend more time there," Charlie had told him. "You don't hire somebody to cut the lawn. *You* cut the lawn. You don't hire a housekeeper. *You* vacuum your own rug; *you* clean your own toilet. Then the house will take on *your* energy." Dale wanted to dismiss his father's advice. He was sitting there at the table in Charlie's kitchen, munching on some homemade peanut brittle Mariah had made as his father pontificated about energy and how to get it in your house. Charlie meandered between the sink and the table, washing a glass, sampling the candy, straightening a few new photos stuck on the refrigerator door with colorful magnets. It suddenly occurred to him: his father was a man at ease in his own skin. In fact, Charlie seemed comfortable wherever he was. Dale didn't buy into Charlie's energy theories, but well, what about *ambience*? That was Jen's favorite word. A conference room, a banquet hall, their own front porch: it all had to convey a certain effect and purpose, a deliberate ambience. But a home—couldn't it just be a home?

Thus began his efforts to convince Jen to slow down with him, to value their careers a little less and their time together a little more. She was five years younger than him. Maybe she hadn't been ready. Maybe if he'd been patient enough to wait. He took another drag on his cigarette. No, he was wise to have let go.

***

"It was nice of you to call," he had concluded, wanting to end the conversation on an even note.

"How are you, Dale?" she said in that drippy voice she got when she was feeling superior. "How are you *really*?"

He snorted impatiently. This is what he got when he let his guard down. "I'm fine, Jen. You know, how do you think I am? It's upsetting, but you know I'm fine. How are you?"

"I'm good, Dale. Work is good. I'm doing okay."

"That's great. Are you engaged yet?"

"Jesus Christ, Dale! I told you that guy I'm seeing--it's not serious, so cut the crap. I called to be nice. I loved Charlie too, you know. He wasn't my father for all that long, but I feel sad about it."

"I know."

And he did know. Jeannette had loved Charlie, and of course Charlie had loved her. She fit in well with his collection of smart and flashy artists and entrepreneurs. Mariah enjoyed her too. After all, Jeannette occasionally took Mariah and her friends on extravagant shopping trips. And Samantha—she was friendly as always—but Dale couldn't help but notice that Samantha was rather quiet when Jeannette was there. Not that she could get a word in edgewise when Charlie and Jeannette were matching wits. But still, Dale wondered later if Samantha saw something he hadn't.

He let the smoke sneak slowly from his mouth, tasting it. The taste of tobacco, it reminded him of her. So often it was on her mouth when he kissed her. He snuffed out the butt on the metal railing, then cradled it in his hand. He refused to dig out an ashtray. That would imply he was making a habit of this. He wasn't going to do that. He just needed it today.

After a quick lunch he went over to his father's house to pick up Hyacinth to drive her to the airport. He'd promised Samantha he'd do that for her. He was sure Aunt Hy was probably getting on his stepmother's nerves. But when he arrived the two of them were thick as thieves, drinking mimosas and eating leftover cold cuts and potato salad from the funeral reception. They looked like they'd been eating and drinking all night, their eyes deeply shadowed and their voices loud and hoarse. Hyacinth was ranting on about how absolutely outstanding it was that Samantha knew all the words to the songs in *The Sound of Music.* "Oh, stop," Samantha giggled. "I do not. But I can sing at least a dozen choruses of the Wheels on the Bus!" They both got really silly about that.

"Are you packed, Aunt Hy?" Dale asked, annoyed at this turn of events.

"Oh, of course, sweetie," she cooed. "My suitcases are

already stacked in the garage."

"But you're not dressed. Where's your traveling suit?"

"Oh, Dale, when in California, you do as the Romans, you know, whatever!" She shook her head and laughed. "I stuffed the suit in one of my vanity cases. Samantha lent me these lovely sweat pants. So much more comfortable than that stiff business suit."

Dale stared at the two of them, wondering what else was going to change. A week ago he could have been sitting in this dining room, laughing with his father about Stephen Colbert's opening monologue or talking about John Grisham's latest novel. And if there were talk of family, Samantha was happy to dish with the best of them. But now his dad was gone, and Sam was besties with his weirdly anachronistic Aunt Hyacinth.

"Where's Mariah?" he asked. "Is she okay? She was still pretty upset when I left last night."

Samantha nodded solemnly. "She's been up half the night scouring the internet for clues about that thimble," Samantha said darkly as she sipped more champagne. "I'm worried about her."

"I'm worried about both of you, Sam," Dale said softly. "I think you both need to get some sleep."

"It just takes time, sweetie," Samantha said, squeezing his arm. "It took time when I lost my parents but I got through it. You and Mariah will be okay too."

"But what about you, Sam? How are you doing?"

"Oh, I'm as good as I'm going to be. I doubt I'll ever really get over this."

Dale's mouth dropped open, unsure what to say to such pessimism, but then Mariah came flying down the hallway. "I've found it," she exclaimed. "My thimble is in Arizona. This man in Arizona is selling my thimble on the internet!"

Dale and Samantha exchanged doubting glances, but Hyacinth shouted for joy. "Oh, Mariah, that's fantastic! Let me see." She rushed down the hall after her teenaged niece.

"What do you think?" Samantha asked Dale.

"I don't know. I suppose it's possible that merchandise could move that quickly, you know, if a thief is experienced and well connected. Still, I don't know how you can be sure that it's *the* thimble. How do you verify something like that? It's not like it has a registration number engraved on the edge."

Mariah reemerged carrying her laptop like a jewel on a pillow. "See look, here it is," she blurted as she thrust the computer toward her mother and brother.

Hyacinth was right at her elbow. "That's it; I'm sure that's it," she babbled, still sporting a flute of orange juice and sparkling wine. She took a hearty gulp. "There's really no doubt."

"Aunt Hy," Dale admonished her, "You cannot be sure that's your oh-so-famous Easter family thimble. That photo looks blurry to me." He was raising his voice now. He could hear the tension in his own tone. He wished there was some way to reel in all this emotion but at that moment he felt out of control.

"Of course I can tell, Dale," Hyacinth said. "You see the tiny little e-shaped eyelid on the right profiled eagle--that's it. That's the distinguishing mark. My grandmother pointed that out to me when I was just a little girl."

"This guy is asking $500 for it," Dale shot back. "That's ridiculous."

"Oh, he's really selling it short, Dale," Hyacinth said smoothly. She sounded as calm as a banker right now, not like his flighty aunt who was three sheets to the wind on champagne and ambrosia salad. "That thimble was appraised at $1200 in January. I have it appraised every year when I renew the insurance," she said, leaning toward Samantha. Samantha nodded, her expression serious.

"So how is this done?" Samantha asked. "I hope we don't have to use a credit card."

"You're going to buy it sight unseen online?" Dale asked incredulously.

"No, of course not," Mariah interjected calmly. "I'm going to Arizona. I've already gone to the Greyhound website to price tickets. I can get a bus to LA tonight, and transfer to Las Vegas, and then--"

"Oh, no, Mariah, I don't think so--" Samantha started.

"Of course not," Hyacinth interrupted. "I'll buy you a plane ticket."

"I was thinking we'd drive," Samantha clarified.

"Are you all crazy?" Dale asked.

Mariah leaned against her brother's arm and graced him with a doe-eyed gaze. "Come with us," she pleaded, resorting to the wiles she'd used since she was barely able to talk. He rolled his eyes.

"Where in Arizona?" Hyacinth asked.

"Sedona," Mariah responded.

"Oh, I've always wanted to see Sedona!" Hyacinth exclaimed. "Can I come too?"

"The more the merrier," Samantha declared.

Dale stepped back, thinking he was surely in some alternate universe. Mariah and Hyacinth had migrated to the table to look up the weather report for Sedona on Mariah's laptop. Then he heard Samantha's soft voice at his left side. "Does your mom still live in Sedona?" she asked, gently touching his shoulder.

Over the years, he had thought of Samantha as mentor, guide, surrogate parent in the absence of his own mother, and finally--in this decade--friend. But first and foremost she was his father's wife, and it had never occurred to him to think of her as seductive. It was not that she seemed sexy, and yet she was suddenly alluring, leading him where he didn't want to go. He didn't want to see his mother right now--did he? Oh, sure, Geneva had been very comforting on the phone when he called to tell her of Charlie's passing, but she hadn't put herself out. Had she thought about Dale and what he was going through? Apparently not. So why should he think about her? He could go see her, but he would come away disappointed. It was inevitable.

"Uh huh, she lives there. Just talked to her last week. She says the weather's pretty nice. I'm sure you'll have a fine trip."

"This would be a good time for you to go visit your mother," Samantha said in a leading tone. She touched his arm. "You know I'm right."

Dale couldn't help but smile at her self assured comment. "How do you figure that?"

"Well," she said with a shrug, "We're all pretty fragile right now. Maybe this trip will be nothing but a diversion. Or maybe it's leading us where we need to go next."

Dale shook his head. "You know I never quite saw the logic in all this energy stuff you and Dad were always talking about. 'Allowing yourself to be led!' I guess I don't know what it means. I've always had to get up and move. Nobody's doing it for me."

"Oh, Dale, it's nothing mysterious. I'm going where the

path leads. I'm not getting a message from on high or something. Mariah wants to go to Arizona, so I'm going to Arizona. Will something significant happen there? Probably not, but it makes Mariah happy. Perhaps on some level my energy is needed there, though I'll probably never understand why. But for you--your sister has invited you on this trip. And where are we going? To the town where your mother lives. That's called synchronicity. There's got to be some purpose in that."

Dale clenched his teeth, unwilling to reveal any emotion. "I'll think about it," he said abruptly as he pulled away from her. "So Aunt Hy, guess you won't be needing a ride to the airport?"

"Not today," she said gleefully. "Oh, I better call my travel agent."

Dale glanced toward the door. "So--my work here is done. I'll talk to you later, Sam."

"Call me tonight, Dale," she called. She reached out to hug him, but he was gone.

***

Alone in his van, Dale pulled out another cigarette. He caught sight of his hands, and stopped himself. His long fingers were so like his mother's.

He did not want to acknowledge that Samantha and her spiritual musings could have some validity. He liked thinking of himself as a free agent, someone who operated on his own authority, who weighed the available evidence and made decisions logically. This crazy blowing in the wind philosophy his dad had espoused didn't sit well with him. But right now, it was hard to escape that he was missing his mother, that he'd been longing to see her and talk to her ever since Samantha had called and told him that Charlie was in an ambulance on the way to the hospital. Why shouldn't he admit that to himself--and to Samantha?

***

Dale offered to do most of the driving, knowing that his van would comfortably fit all four of them and their luggage. "Just promise me you won't let Hyacinth mix any more drinks," he told Samantha. "You begin to remind me of her after a few swallows."

Samantha smiled. "I don't know, Dale," she said. "I think I've had more influence on her than the other way around." Hyacinth emerged dressed in new jeans, moccasins, and a T-shirt that read "Goddess on the Loose."

Samantha lowered her voice to whisper to Dale. "Hy went on a shopping spree at the first mention of a road trip. Wait till you see the collection of junk food she's picked up. We will not want for salt in the desert."

***

When Geneva heard Dale and the women were coming to Sedona she insisted that her son bring Charlie's family to stay with her. Samantha seemed reticent at the idea, but Hyacinth seemed to assume she was a welcome addition to any household. "I can't wait to see your mother again, Dale," she said as they pulled onto the freeway in Sacramento. "We met a few times, oh so long ago! The first time was Charlie's graduation from Dartmouth. Such a pretty campus. Have you ever been to New Hampshire, Samantha? So lovely with deep dark woods. But then, surely you know Geneva well, don't you Sam?"

"No, not well," Samantha said. "We met a few times back when Charlie and I were first together. When Dale was still in elementary school."

74

"She always liked you," Dale assured her.

"Well, of course, she liked me," Samantha blurted. "I took Charlie off her hands!" Then she gasped, realizing that she'd just made a disparaging remark about her late husband in front of his two children. Hyacinth laughed, but Mariah turned in her seat to give her mother a surprised glare.

"Gee, Mom," the teenager said.

"She's right, Mariah," Dale told her. "Our father wasn't always easy to handle."

Mariah scrunched down in the seat and said nothing. Hyacinth began singing *Sunrise, Sunset* from *Fiddler on the Roof,* but Samantha shushed her. "Not that one," she said with mock exaggeration.

"How bout this: 'Raindrops on roses, and whiskers on kittens--'"

"Bright copper kettles and warm woolen mittens," Mariah joined in.

Samantha sighed with relief and stared out the window as they headed south.

Chapter Six

The newness of their loss, the sudden decision to travel, and the addition of Hyacinth to their small number gave the trip a sense of novelty, even festiveness. Samantha and Hyacinth kept up a steady flow of chatter, relating family histories and tall tales. Hyacinth delighted in leading the group in song, particularly show tunes and standards from the 40s and 50s. Samantha preferred the more singable folk songs of Pete Seeger and Peter, Paul and Mary. Dale and Mariah joined in when they turned to the music of James Taylor and Carol King. No one said so, but Samantha knew the common link was because JT and King were Charlie's favorites.

When they tired of singing, Samantha kept them busy with word and number games she often played with her students. Dale surprised them by reciting a Robert Frost poem he'd memorized in high school as well as two Billy Collins pieces he'd learned to please Jeannette. His performance reminded her so much of Charlie that Samantha nearly sobbed, but she managed to staunch her tears in silence and Dale, his eyes on the road, never knew.

As promised, Dale did most of the driving. Hyacinth begged off, claiming the unfamiliarity of the road and the size of the vehicle were too daunting for her. Mariah had had her driver's license for less than a year. No one asked her to drive and she didn't offer. But Samantha took a turn every day, giving Dale a welcome relief.

***

They arrived in Sedona midafternoon of the third day. Geneva and her husband lived in a large adobe-styled mansion nestled in an elevated cul de sac with stunning views of red rock formations on all sides. She greeted the travelers straight from her garden: her T-shirt looked frayed and the knees of her khaki pants were stained with reddish mud. She pulled off a floppy sun hat to display white hair cut in a pageboy framing her square face. She was tall and imposing, but still beautiful with her dark eyes and direct manner. "Welcome, welcome!" she exclaimed, reaching out with both hands to Samantha and Hyacinth. "I am so sorry for your loss. And this must be Mariah, the daughter of Charlie Easter! I'm so happy to finally meet the sister of my own son. Thank you for enriching his life, Mariah!"

Mariah was speechless at the exuberant words of this unfamiliar woman. Looking up at her as she embraced Dale warmly, it occurred to her for the first time that she had seen few photos of Dale's mother. She had never seen any displayed in his house or condo, and her father had had few photos of the past. Samantha was the family photographer: there were dozens of albums as well as computer files filled with the documentation of Samantha's life and the people she loved. But Charlie and Dale seemed to have had no such interest in preserving memories.

Geneva ushered them in, offered them food and drink. She brought in homemade flat bread and honey butter served with green leaf tea or iced coffee. Geneva explained that her husband was away for the week, serving as a legal consultant to the Navajo Nation. Mariah listened as her mother and aunt were gracious and chatty, talking about the trip and the weather, finally easing into stories of her father, the funeral, the theft. Then Geneva took them to their rooms.

Dale stayed in a guesthouse in the back as he had at every visit since he was a teenager. Samantha and Mariah shared a king sized bed in a spacious guest room, but Hyacinth was once again offered a space in an office. This office was huge with a fireplace, leather furniture and fold-out couch. Hyacinth found it very comfortable.

Settled in their room, Mariah began to unpack. She gently pulled out the box that held her great grandmother's dresser set, and lay the comb, brush and mirror on the vanity table. Next she pulled out the crystal apple that she had nestled amid T-shirts and balled up socks. "Oh my goodness, Mariah," her mother exclaimed. "Why did you bring all that?"

"For strength, Mom," Mariah answered in a tone reflexively defensive. "I need the treasures of the Easter family with me to give me strength. You understand, don't you?"

"I guess," Samantha said in a tone that indicated she did not understand at all. Her mother sank onto the bed behind her, yet somehow Mariah could feel her mother's gaze focused on her back. She picked up the silver comb and drew it through her long hair. She felt a gulf had opened between her mother and herself. Of course Mariah realized she could not fully understand her mother's pain at losing her husband. But her mother could not understand what it meant to Mariah to learn she'd had a twin. Somehow this new knowledge had set her on a path she felt compelled to follow. She wanted to tell her mother about it, she wanted to share it with her, but she didn't know how to put it into words.

There was a knock on the door, then silence as Geneva politely waited to be invited in. Mariah opened the door, but still Geneva stood beyond the threshold. "Can I get you anything? Towels or toiletries? Everything you need to bathe or shower should be in the bathroom, but please don't hesitate to ask."

"Thank you so much, Geneva," Samantha said. "We so appreciate your hospitality."

"I'm the one who should be thanking you," Geneva

interjected, "for bringing Dale home to me. I was second guessing myself, thinking that perhaps I should have come to Charlie's funeral--you know, for Dale's sake. But I didn't want—well, you understand, Samantha. He was *your* husband."

Samantha stood and nodded. "I do understand--and I'm very grateful that you've welcomed us now."

Geneva nodded. "Well, we'll be serving dinner in about an hour, so that should give you a chance to relax, and--oh--" She glanced down at the vanity where Mariah had laid the brush, comb and mirror. "Is that Melora Easter's dresser set?"

Mariah nodded proudly. "Yes, it belonged to my great-grandmother."

"You're familiar with it, I see," Samantha said.

"It's so funny, and actually very dear," Geneva explained. "You know, Mariah, your Aunt Hyacinth used to travel with the dresser set too. She used to take it with her wherever she went. I remember her coming to visit us when we were students in New Hampshire, and again when we lived in California, and there would be the dresser set, spread out in our guest room, or even on a Formica table top in the cheap motel room--the only one we could afford to rent for her back then. I think it had a special magic for her as it apparently does for you now."

"Yes!" Mariah exclaimed. "That's it exactly."

Geneva smiled wryly, narrowing her eyes. "And yet you seem to be--uh, quite different from your aunt. Perhaps this dresser set has a power I myself do not detect."

Mariah shrugged. "I guess so."

Mariah saw Geneva catch her mother's eye and smile. She wondered if Geneva thought her decision to bring the dresser set with her was cute or even silly, an affectation of some kind. And yet, her father had once loved Geneva. She was in fact the first woman he had ever loved. She must be special. Surely Geneva wouldn't belittle her.

***

In the morning Mariah and her mother, her aunt and her brother set out to meet the man who had advertised the thimble on e-bay. The man had expressed surprise that they had wanted to come receive the thimble in person, rather than allowing him to mail it to them. "Hey, it's your nickel," he told Dale on the phone. "Come on by the shop when you get to town."

Owen Redheels owned an unusual little hole in the wall shop on the outskirts of Sedona in a strip mall that housed a tire shop, a T shirt store, and a place that sold Catholic medals, rosaries and statuary. A police car was parked in front of Redheels' Antiques and Collectables. "I wonder why the police are here," Mariah said in a fearful voice.

Dale laughed and pointed to a donut shop two doors down. Mariah hoped her brother was right, but she was too anxious to laugh. They went inside.

The shop was filled with carved wooden animals, burl wood coffee tables, plenty of knickknacks, and salt and pepper shakers. A balding red haired man with a New York accent was apparently just finishing his conversation with the police officer. At their appearance the officer went off to the back of the store, while the other man greeted them. "Good morning, can I help you?"

"Dale Easter," Dale extended his hand. "We spoke a few days ago about a thimble with hawks engraved on it. This is my sister Mariah, my Aunt Hyacinth and my stepmother Samantha."

"Gosh, you're the folks from California," Redheels said

80

looking rather forlorn at their appearance. "You come all this way and jeez, I feel so bad--"

"Why?" Mariah asked desperately.

Redheels shook his head sadly. "C'mere--you gotta see this."

He led them from the more rustic looking part of the shop through a narrow corridor to a larger room in the back. This room was as lush as any jewelry store with polished glass display cases boasting antique rings and bracelets, diamonds, rubies and sapphires lined up in neat rows, rare coins, and precious figurines. "Now you see, this part of the store is where I keep the more--you know--expensive items. Here's where I've got the stuff that needs protection, and well, I'm not going to give away any secrets, suffice to say that I've got these cases wired up nice and secure. But the thimble wasn't in these here cases. No, I'd sold that to you, so it was no longer on display. So I had it here in the back. C'mere, I'll show ya." He led them behind the far counter to an office with a kitchenette and a door apparently leading to a small patio with a picnic table. "See here," he said. "This is what I was just showing the police officers. Here's my safe: someone came in here and blew it right open! Used some kind of plastic explosive--can you believe that? All I've got in here--three items awaiting pick-up by the purchasers--but the only one they touched was your thimble. And no offense, but that thimble was the least valuable item in there."

"Don't be so sure about that, buster," Hyacinth jumped in. "You were underselling that thimble. It was worth a lot more than you thought."

"Well, obviously, ma'am, you're right, it had some worth to somebody, because they took that thimble and--"

"They took my thimble?" Mariah exclaimed. "But it was *my* thimble!"

"That's right, miss, they took your thimble and they left behind a two caret diamond ring and a pair of ruby earrings. So your aunt here is right. That thimble was sure worth a helluva lot to somebody." He paused. "And you folks were willing to drive all the way here from northern California, so it meant something to you too. What's the story?"

"I can't believe this," Mariah cried out, beginning to sob. Samantha pulled her daughter into her arms, and Hyacinth wrapped an arm around the two of them.

"What is going on here?" Dale said, puffing himself up for combat. "Is this some kind of scam?"

"Over a collectable thimble?" Owen asked incredulously. "You gotta be kidding. Maybe you didn't hear me--I've got a two-caret diamond in that safe. I've got plenty of stuff like that in here. That thimble--sure it was nice, rather unusual, and it had a bit of the southwest flavor to it--what with the hawks and all--"

"Those are eagles engraved on there, Mister," Hyacinth chimed in indignantly.

"Whatever, Lady, you call 'em whatever you like. My point is I don't often carry merchandise like that. Thimbles--not a big market for something like that. If I was going to scam somebody--and I'm not in the business of scamming nobody-- well, it sure wouldn't be over some little thimble."

Mariah stood stunned, her arms still wrapped around her mother, hearing, but not fully comprehending, the voices of her aunt and brother arguing with the shopkeeper. She felt like a helpless child, a mere by-stander on this stage. The movie was playing but she was only a spectator.

"Listen," Redheels was saying, "I'm awful sorry; I sure didn't mean to disappoint you--but do you folks know what's going on here?'

"We don't know either," her mother said as she rubbed Mariah's back.

Dale stepped forward and answered in a low voice. Mariah could barely hear him. "My father just died--less than two weeks ago--and well, the thimble meant a lot to my sister."

Owen rubbed his chin. "You talk as if this thimble belonged to you in the first place--

"This thimble has been in the Easter family for over a hundred and fifty years," Hyacinth informed him in her haughtiest tone. "It was forged by a goldsmith in Massachusetts after it was commissioned by our great-great-great-grandfather."

"Okay," Owen said dismissively, as if to say TMI! "But," he continued, "I got this thimble from a reliable source. This woman has never brought me stolen material before. I trust her."

"Could we talk to her?" Dale asked. "We'd really like to find the thimble for my sister. Maybe she has some ideas."

"Sure, I'll give you her name and number," Owen said. "You may as well talk to her. It's unlikely the police are going find it. I only filed a report so I could make an insurance claim. But they're not going to bust their butts looking for it."

Mariah felt slapped. "Why not?" she asked as she pulled away from her mother. "Why are the police officers in every city so impotent?"

Dale looked at her in mild surprise and gave her a comical smirk. "Where'd you learn that word?" he asked.

"No joking now, Dale," she chastised him. "Not now. Besides you know it's the right word!"

Owen nodded vigorously. "The little girl is right. That is the right word to describe all our traditional authority figures these days. Impotent! You got that right, sweetheart." He paused after this pronouncement to shake his head, but Mariah felt stung again. He had called her a little girl.

"What I don't understand," Redheels continued in a suddenly contemplative way, "is how this person knew where to look for the thimble. And it seems pretty obvious they got what they came for now, doesn't it? But you see, I never had the thimble on display at all. It was on e-bay for less than a day and you contacted me and I put it right in the safe to wait for you. When I got it, I put it in a drawer with the new merchandise for cleaning—"

"But I just had it professionally cleaned when I decided to bring it to California to give to Mariah," Hyacinth interrupted. "It shouldn't have needed cleaning."

"Okay, lady, that's fine, it looked clean enough," Owen assured her. "I always clean the new merchandise whether it needs it or not—it's something I do routinely--you know--so it all looks good--and has a uniformly shiny appearance. But my point is--how would anyone have known? This is a very strange case here."

"There's something very bizarre about all this," Samantha said softly. "There's some kind of unusual energy about the thimble. It's attracting some very strange people and events."

"Energy," Dale said simply. But Mariah had heard her brother and father arguing on spiritual themes in the past. She knew Dale's one-word comment was a cynical challenge.

"Mom is right," Mariah told him quickly.

"Well," he said, spreading his hands in surrender. "I can't argue with her. None of this makes any sense."

Chapter Seven

Mariah sat alone at the big oak table in Geneva's dining room. The night before the table had been clothed in peach-colored linens and topped with a vase of orange and yellow asters. Today the table was bare and unadorned.

Determined to focus on the here and now as her mother had taught her to do when she was upset, Mariah took a deep breath. She deliberately flexed the fingers of her right hand, then gently pushed her palm down on to the table top. It was a solid piece of blond wood, round with a wide circumference: eight or ten people could probably squeeze around its rim. It stood on a claw-footed pedestal, and Mariah wondered if it was an antique. Or perhaps its tiny nicks and stains had been earned here in Geneva's care. Had she brought this table with her from California? Was this the table where Dale sat to eat breakfast when he was in grade school? Did her father once sit at this table with baby Dale in his arms?

Soft laughter drifted in from the kitchen and Mariah lifted her head. She swallowed hard, then rose to join the others in the next room.

Standing quietly in the doorway, Mariah saw Geneva measuring herbs into a teapot. Her mother stood at a cutting board slicing corn bread onto a crockery plate. Hyacinth was unabashedly going through the cupboards as if evaluating the quality of Geneva's china. She chose a small dish and turned to hand it to Samantha. "We can put the jam on this, Sam." She caught sight of Mariah then and took a step toward her. "Take a look at this, honey," she invited, holding the dish out to her niece. "Isn't it precious?"

It was a shallow bowl with a bird painted on it. "We have one like this at home," Mariah said.

"Do you?" Hyacinth asked.

"Yes, this is a ruby-throated hummingbird." She looked to her mother for confirmation but Samantha was looking at Geneva. The two women exchanged a smile, but both appeared unsurprised.

Dale entered through the far door, clearing his throat as he stared at his sister across the room. "I tried calling the woman Redheels said sold him the thimble. The number's been disconnected. I tried googling her—zilch. And the thimble is not on e-bay. Not yet anyway."

Mariah felt her throat tighten and she clenched her teeth, trying to keep from crying again. Suddenly her mother was there, enfolding her in her arms, and she surrendered to tears. The room was silent except for the faint pinging of metal on china as Hyacinth spooned strawberry jam onto the hummingbird plate.

Mariah pulled away from Samantha. "I'm okay," she whispered. Samantha took her hand and led her daughter into the kitchen, gesturing toward a stool at the counter near where she was slicing bread. Mariah sat obediently. Dale squeezed her shoulder as he took a seat beside her. "Sorry, Mare," he murmured.

Geneva stepped away from her post near the teakettle warming on the stove. "Mariah," she said in a loud, distinct voice. "Can you tell me: why is the thimble so important to you?"

Surprised by the sudden question, Mariah sat up

straighter, feeling like a student caught unprepared. "I don't know," she blurted, dismayed at how much like a little girl she sounded. "It just is."

Geneva leaned toward her across the counter. "You know, dear, when you go on a quest, it's very important to be able to articulate your goals and your motives."

Mariah stared at Geneva, leaning back in her chair, unsure what to say. Dale leaned forward abruptly, angling his shoulder her way, as if shielding his sister from his mother. "Mariah doesn't think of it that way, Mom. It has sentimental value to her. That's not easy to define."

Geneva moved easily back toward the stove. "Of course it's not easy, Dale," she said in a friendly, almost neutral way. "But sometimes it's the next step on the path."

Dale snorted and Mariah could see he was annoyed. Samantha placed a hand on his forearm and spoke in her calming teacher voice. "I think your mother is right, Dale," she said. "It is important for Mariah to re-examine her goal." Mariah exhaled now, relieved to see her mother enter the fray, playing peacemaker as she often felt compelled to do. She continued. "The path on the physical plane appears to have disappeared. The next step must be within. It's the only choice. And what better way to begin than by asking why? Why is this thimble important? Why do you need it? What does it give to you? And if you can't find the thimble, then what can you find to replace what it provides? The energy it gives you."

"Energy again," Dale said dismissively. He stood suddenly, picked up napkins and placemats and headed toward the dining room with them. His mother followed, calling after him in her professorial voice.

"Oh Dale, Samantha has summed it up perfectly. Much better than I could." Dale shrugged as he eased past her to pick up the mugs Hyacinth had chosen. Geneva continued.

"I hardly need to say this aloud," she said slowly, her head lowered, "but perhaps it would do our hearts good to acknowledge tonight that we have all lost something--someone--important to us, and it will take a long time to realize how we will deal with that loss. How we can replace the energy that Charlie provided--if that energy even *can* be replaced. And if it can't be replaced then how can we make ourselves whole without it?"

Mariah saw her mother's eyes were filled with tears. "Thank you, Geneva," she said. "That was also well said."

Dale paused in the doorway, the hummingbird plate filled with jam in his hand. "Yeah, nicely put, Mom," he agreed though his voice dripped sarcasm. "And you include yourself here, among those grieving a loss?"

Geneva faced her son squarely. "I do, Dale. And I know you've come all this way to challenge me on this point, to somehow express your anger that I didn't love your father better, that I couldn't stay with him the way you would have liked when you were a child, that I couldn't have given you the wonderful family your sister had with Charlie and Samantha."

"That's not true," he retorted. "That's not what I wanted."

"If you were honest with yourself--"

"I'm not the one being dishonest!"

The teakettle emitted a shrill whistle, and every head turned, momentarily diverted away from the rising argument. "I'll get it!" Hyacinth cried. She scooped up a quilted oven mitt and leapt toward the stove in one swift motion to move the kettle from the hot burner to a cool one. Why isn't she making the tea? Mariah wondered, thinking that a well-timed snack would ease this uncomfortable tension. But Aunt Hy had turned, oven mitt clenched in both hands near her heart, enthralled by the mother/son drama unfolding in the doorway, eager to hear more. Mariah turned too but reluctantly, lifting her eyes cautiously to see what might happen next.

"Oh, Dale, I don't want to argue with you." Geneva stopped then, and took the plate of jam from him, setting it on the counter. She cleared her throat and began again in a softer voice. "Please know this: I did love your father!--and although I've had little contact with him for decades, of course he meant a lot to me, and I mourn his passing. Of course I do. Don't you realize? Nothing I have done in my life, nothing I have achieved is more important to me than you. And if I hadn't fallen in love with Charlie, I would have no son." She finally reached forward then, daring to touch his hand. "My life is unthinkable without you. Don't you know that?"

Dale stared down at the floor, apparently unable to speak.

Geneva's voice cracked. "I am so sorry if I haven't made that clear to you over the years. I am so sorry."

Dale shook his head and spoke in a voice choked with emotion. "It's okay, Mom; I know."

Geneva nodded, squeezing Dale's hand and swinging it to affect a less emotional demeanor. "So," she said, twirling around to face the other women, "is the tea ready?"

"What?" Hyacinth asked.

"The tea, Hy!" Samantha said, stifling a laugh. She handed the plate of corn bread to Mariah, gesturing toward the doorway, and Mariah rose. Hyacinth poured water into the teapot. All picked up mugs and serving plates, readying for a migration to the dining room.

"Can we still go hiking tomorrow?" Mariah asked as she set the corn bread on the table.

"Of course," Samantha said and there was a general murmur of agreement.

"I hope you don't plan to go hiking in those shoes, Mariah,"

Geneva said pointing to her thin-soled but stylish high-top sneakers.

Feeling embarrassed to be singled out by Geneva again, Mariah sat quickly. "These have always been fine before," she said defensively.

Samantha leaned back to look at her daughter's shoes. "You didn't pack your hiking boots?" she asked as she seated herself next to her daughter.

"These are fine, Mom. Besides I didn't have room for my boots."

"You had room for the dresser set and apple," Hyacinth chimed in, "but you didn't have room for your boots?" Mariah shrugged, staring at her hands.

Geneva stood at the head of the table as the others seated themselves. "When you are on a quest, Mariah," she said gently, "it is important to be prepared. You need good boots." She poured a mug of tea and passed it to Dale to be delivered. "I would be happy to take you to a shop I know of in town tomorrow and get you a pair of very fine leather boots for your journey."

"Oh, Geneva," Samantha exclaimed as she accepted a mug of tea from Dale. "That is much too generous of you."

Geneva smiled as she handed Dale another mug. "You misunderstand me, Samantha. I cannot give the boots to your daughter. She will have to pay me for them."

Samantha drew back in her chair, embarrassed and confused. Dale stood frozen next to his mother, staring down at the mug of liquid she had handed him. Geneva continued.

"These boots are very special, hand made in fact. I know that Mariah could find some that are cheaper in any shoe store in town. But I will trade them for Melora's dresser set."

Dale set the mug of tea in front of Mariah, splashing a bit of the hot liquid onto the table. Mariah gasped softly, reaching to mop it up with a paper napkin. "You can't take Mariah's dresser set," he shouted. "Hyacinth just gave those to her. They belonged to our great-grandmother."

"I know that, Dale. Hyacinth showed me Melora's lovely set years ago. I think this would be a good trade."

"I don't even know what to say," Dale blurted again. "I have never known you to be so crass!"

"Dale--" Samantha cautioned, but he cut her off.

"No, Sam, I don't get it," he retorted. "This isn't like her."

Geneva lowered her eyes as she slowly and deliberately poured another cup of tea. "Your sister is on a quest, Dale," she said finally as she set the cup on the table. "When you're on a quest it's important to understand that knowledge comes at a price." Without missing a beat, she poured another mug, then turned to Dale. "Sacrifice is required."

Dale waved away the mug his mother offered him. "I've heard enough of this quest garbage, and what's important to understand," he said. "This is all a crock."

"No, wait, Dale," Samantha interjected herself again. "Think about it," she continued as she patted the empty chair between herself and Geneva, urging him to sit. "When you're on a quest, sacrifice is required. That is true, and it's been true for millennia. Every archetypal story affirms that you can't get something for nothing. It's simple economics." She paused, again gesturing toward the chair.

Dale surrendered with a snort to sit beside his stepmother. "But still--" he began.

"I know," Samantha interrupted. "Let me finish." She turned toward her daughter. "Mariah, only you can decide if this search for the thimble is indeed a quest. Only you can decide if the boots are needed in your quest. This is your story, baby. You write it however you like."

Mariah had been watching the discussion like a spectator at a tennis match. Was it time for her to enter the game? Her breath was shallow, so she drew some air down deep into into her belly. "I, uh--" She hesitated, realizing that the first words out of her mouth were going to be *I don't know.* She said that often, she knew that she did. It was a habit like *oh, you know.* The time to rely on such unproductive habits was over. She squared back her shoulders and lifted her head to face Geneva. "I want to thank you," she said, "for helping me realize--um--helping me realize how rudderless I've been. I mean--Yes! That's exactly what I mean to say. I've been drifting, pulling my family down here to Arizona, searching, for what?--I couldn't even tell you why it was important, but now I feel it's time for a gesture--to uh--signal to the universe that I'm serious, that this is a true quest." She paused again. "Okay," she continued with a nod. "The dresser set means a lot to me. I don't want to trade it."

"Good," Dale said with a sigh.

"I don't want to," Mariah repeated. "But I will give you the comb."

"What?" Dale exclaimed.

"Ha!" Geneva exploded with a short burst of laughter. "Oh your sister is much more clever than I had expected."

"Mariah," Hyacinth pleaded, "you can't break up the set!"

"She is bargaining with me--that's a good thing," Geneva admonished Hyacinth. "Let her do what she will." She turned back to Mariah. "The comb is not nearly enough, Mariah. But I will settle for the mirror."

"Oh, no," Mariah responded immediately. "It's important I

keep the mirror. I know it's only symbolic but--" she looked toward her mother, "You know what I mean, Mom."

"It symbolizes the desire to go within, to search the soul," Samantha agreed. "You're right to keep the mirror."

"I'll give you the brush," Mariah told Geneva.

"The brush and the comb both?" Geneva countered.

Mariah nodded immediately. "Deal."

"I can't believe this," Dale exclaimed. "Samantha, you can't allow this."

Mariah held her breath, watching Dale appeal to her mother. She knew this was hard for her brother, and her aunt too: it was tempting to reverse her decision for their sakes, to decline Geneva's offer of the boots. But she knew her time had come to assert herself.

"I'm sorry, Dale," Samantha was saying, "but you and I can't interfere. This is Mariah's journey; we have no say in it."

Mariah exhaled, picking up her mug of tea and taking a hasty gulp. She said a silent prayer of gratitude that her mother understood and was willing to back her.

But Dale wasn't finished. "Well," he said, "maybe as representative of the Easter family, I need to put my foot down and say this won't happen, mother. You can't treat my sister this way."

"Dale!" his mother exclaimed as she fingered her own mug. "It will be okay, your sister has proved herself to be both clever *and* wise. She bargained with me, and kept what she knew intuitively was the most important piece, the mirror. She didn't bow to my demand to give me the dresser set. She rose to the occasion." Geneva turned and lifted her mug in a salute to Mariah. "Kudos, my dear!"

Mariah nodded, feeling shy again, but allowing herself a small smile. "Thank you," she murmured.

Geneva then lifted her mug toward Mariah's mother. "She is a credit to you, Samantha. You raised her well."

Samantha smiled sadly. "Charlie and I raised her well. Together we raised her well."

Geneva nodded, finally seating herself, signaling that they should help themselves to corn bread. "You see, Dale," Geneva said, "there is a kinship among the women who loved Charlie Easter. It is not a kinship we chose, but it has created a bond among us nonetheless."

Dale sat with his forearms resting on the table's edge, his fist clenched. "I loved him too," he shot back, "and I can tell you this is not what he wanted for Mariah."

"I'm sure you're right," Geneva conceded, as she dared to place a slice of corn bread on Dale's plate. "This is not what Charlie would have wanted for his daughter. He would have wanted to protect his little girl, because Charlie was a man like all men who want to do that for their children. But Charlie knew what the spirit requires. He understood what it was to be on a quest."

Dale stared at the corn bread as if it had offended him. "I don't think he would have been happy--"

"Dale," Geneva interrupted. "Your father loved you so much. He fought hard to be a good father to you."

Dale looked up abruptly, apparently surprised. "What do you mean--he fought hard?"

Geneva nibbled on a morsel of bread, looking thoughtful. "I mean that he had to fight his random nature. He used to call it his 'serpentine nature.'"

"Yes," Samantha agreed.

Geneva took a quick sip of tea. "He had a hard time following a straight line, surrendering to a routine. He wanted to get up in the morning and wander--that's all--he wanted to go for a walk and follow his fancy. He didn't want to show up at a job every day at the same time. He wanted to let the universe lead him to a mountain or a meadow or down to the river for a swim. If he saw an interesting person, he wanted to sit down and talk to him or her. He didn't want to worry about showing up for dinner at 6 o'clock. But he showed up for you, Dale. He loved you fiercely."

Dale seemed calmer now, taking a bite of corn bread. "He called me nearly every night when I was growing up," he remembered, "and he was there to take me out every Sunday. That wasn't so difficult for him."

"Exactly," Geneva said, "he was there. But don't think that wasn't difficult for him. He did it for you because he loved you so much. But please understand that Samantha and I knew things about him that you didn't. It's the way the world works. Parents cannot reveal their full selves to their children. Not initially anyway."

"Mom," Dale blurted, spreading his hands. "I knew he was homeless back then. That's no surprise."

Mariah felt a stab of panic in her throat. She turned to face her brother. "He was homeless?"

Samantha reached out quickly and took her daughter's hand. "Yes, that's true," she confirmed. "Your dad was homeless. For several years actually."

Mariah pulled her hand back. "Well, it's because he liked to camp," she said tentatively. "He liked to go sleep outside in his sleeping bag in the backyard all the time. Just two weeks ago he was out sleeping under the redwood tree. That's probably why, don't you think?"

Mariah could see her mother look toward Geneva. The two

women were exchanging guarded glances and nods. Samantha took a deep breath. "When I first met your father," she said slowly. "I told myself that it didn't matter that he was homeless. He seemed very resourceful and never slept on the street. He always slept at friends' houses or in their back yards. Sometimes he camped by the river. And I told myself he liked this life style, that he had chosen it. But the fact is, Mariah, what I learned is that no one chooses that kind of life. Not in this culture. People who are chronically homeless--it happens for a reason."

Mariah gripped the edge of the table, attempting to steady her emotion. "Are you saying there was something wrong with Daddy?" she blurted.

Samantha laid her palm on Mariah's back. "He became much more settled in later years, and we made a good life together, didn't we, Mariah? And he did it out of love for you and for me. We had a good life."

Mariah lifted herself in her chair. "Is this what you all think?" she challenged the group. "Do you all think there was something wrong with Daddy?"

Dale cleared his throat. "We can't know for sure, Mariah, but there was *something* going on. I don't know what," he acknowledged.

"We always called him quirky, you know, when we were growing up," Hyacinth said.

Mariah could hold it in no longer; a sob escaped from her throat. As she let her head sink onto her arms, she heard her mother's chair scraping on the floor. "I know it's a lot more than you wanted to know, baby," Mariah heard her mother whisper as she wrapped her arms around Mariah's shoulders. "I'm sorry."

"When you are on a quest," Geneva began in a gentle tone. "You have opened your heart to the universe and all kinds of knowledge comes flooding in. A lot of this information is very hard to swallow. But it's knowledge that you need or it wouldn't come to you. That you can be sure of."

"Enough of this crap about quests, Mom, okay?" Dale said in an annoyed voice.

"Dale!" Geneva exclaimed, abandoning her serene facade. "Your father loved you so much and I know you loved him, but you resisted the one thing he so wanted to give you: a spiritual core. He was a man in love with ritual and ceremony as a way to approach the divine. But you rejected this. He was, in his way, a mystic."

"He was also a man in love with the Earth," Dale countered. "And that is what he gave to me. He took me camping and kayaking and taught me to care for what is real, what I can see and feel with my own two hands."

Geneva nodded, apparently humbled. "I'm grateful that he gave you something I couldn't. I gave up so much when I left the res. I wanted to live in a nice house, and work in a nice office. I wanted to wear silk suits and high heels and be as good as any white man--and that's what I did, eventually. But what did I do my first year out at college--I fell in love with a coyote trickster named Charlie Easter. Now his daughter has come to remind me of a different side of myself with her hunger and her desire to learn and to seek. I hope you'll let your sister's example open your heart too, Dale. I love you, and I want this for you."

***

Samantha lay awake in the king size bed listening as Mariah's breathing slowed and she drifted off to sleep. Her own mind was racing and she knew she would sleep little this night. Then she smelled the distinct odor of cigarette smoke and she turned to see the silhouetted shadow of her stepson on the patio outside her window. She sat up, pulled a sweatshirt over her nightgown and went out to join him.

He was sitting at a long wrought iron table and he jumped up when he heard her approaching. "Well, you've caught me," he said, lifting the hand that held the cigarette. "Kind of a shock, I guess."

"No, Dale," she said wearily, "I've been smelling tobacco on your clothes ever since your dad died. I know you're doing what you need to do to cope. It's okay."

He held the cigarette away from her as if that would shield her from the wayward traveling smoke. "Sorry," he said briefly. "I don't mean to be so short."

"None of us do. It comes with the territory right now."

"Yeah."

"Are you okay?" she asked.

He shrugged. "I've lost my father and I'm mad as hell at my mother," he stated flatly. "Not a great place to be."

"I know."

"Do you?" he shot back.

"Okay, I don't know!" she replied. "But I'd like to know, and that's something."

Dale lifted his hands abruptly as if signaling surrender and a proximity light popped on, casting a harsh glare on their corner of the yard. He rolled his eyes. "Shit," he cursed softly. "Didn't mean to do that."

Samantha gaped at the size of the guesthouse a few hundred feet down a gravel path. "Wow," she whispered. "I think that's bigger than the town house I bought before I married your dad."

Dale looked embarrassed again, lifting his shoulders to shield his face as he took another drag on his cigarette.

"Lawyer money," he mumbled apologetically, and Samantha felt guilty she'd said anything.

"I'm sorry. I didn't mean--"

"No, hey, don't be sorry," he said, waving his hand at the smoke. "Come take a look."

He headed up the path, then turned to wait for her to catch up. She hastened to his side and he lowered his voice. "Sam," he said, "I feel so bad I blurted out that Dad was homeless."

"That was hardly a secret—

"It was to Mariah!" he lamented, as he stepped onto the narrow porch. "I wasn't thinking."

Samantha squeezed his hand before he could reach for the doorknob. "It's good not to think sometimes," she said as if this pronouncement could only be delivered on a threshold. "It's good to be impulsive and speak your mind out loud. It's like your mother said--if Mariah didn't need that information it wouldn't come to her. That's the way the universe works."

"Maybe it is, maybe you all are right," he admitted as he pulled away to snuff out his cigarette. "I don't think Mariah needed that information today, this very minute, while she's still coming to term with Dad's death." He cradled the spent butt in his palm. "I feel cruel to have laid that on her plate."

Samantha sighed, but she wanted to slap him. She wanted to tell him that all this guilt and blame was another form of self-pity--and good God, snap out of it! But to say that would make *her* feel cruel: it was too soon for that.

He opened the door and leaned in, gesturing for her to precede him into the house. "Welcome to my home away from home."

She forced a smile, her thoughts elsewhere, eager for the tour to be quick and uneventful. Then he flipped on the light and she gasped. The small house did indeed remind her of the place she bought nearly twenty years ago, just weeks before Charlie re-entered her life. Blue and brown Mexican tile covered the floor, the couch and armchair were leather with teal throws and pillows, and prints of Georgia O'Keefe flowers graced the walls.

"You all right?" Dale asked as he deposited his cigarette butt in a small wood stove near the couch.

She laughed. "I guess it never occurred to me that your father had a type."

He closed the door and motioned for her to sit down. "What do you mean?"

She ignored his invitation to sit and spread her arms in the center of the room. "This looks so much like my old house it's spooky."

He shook his head as he flopped down in the leather chair. "Don't worry about it. Mom has a decorator."

"Oh," she murmured, still standing.

He sat up and leaned forward. "I'm sorry, Sam. Would you rather go back to bed? Or I could get you something to drink? And I think there's cheese and crackers in the kitchen if you're hungry."

"No, no, I'm fine," she said finally sinking down to perch on the edge of the couch, still looking around the room. "I was just thinking--"

She paused and he raised his eyebrows. "About--?"

She turned to face him squarely. "I want to tell you something I've never told anyone else before," she whispered.

He looked up at her, his mouth open, his chin lowered, apparently startled by her offer of a revelation. She wanted to laugh, to assure him he could handle it, but he was already nodding. "Okay," he told her.

She swallowed and took a deep breath. "Tonight we all admitted that we have wondered and worried over the years about Charlie's mental health," she began slowly.

He jumped in quickly. "I think you cured him these last eighteen years. He was much steadier, less impulsive, more settled--I mean he was--"

"Oh, gosh, Dale," she blurted, nearly bursting into tears, "you know I couldn't have cured him! It doesn't work that way. That's not what I wanted to talk about."

"Oh, okay." He leaned back, folding his fingers patiently in his lap. "So what is it?"

She noticed a burl wood coffee table in front of her and leaned forward to run her index finger along the wood grain. "You see," she said, her gaze focused on the table, "over the years, I wondered, and of course I'll never know now for sure, but well--" She paused to look up at him. "I came to believe that your father might have been on the autism spectrum."

Dale's head reared back. "You think he was autistic? I can't see that--"

"Hear me out," she pleaded. "I think he had Asperger's Syndrome, or High Functioning Autism."

"I'm not sure--"

Samantha lifted her hands, palms out like stop signs. "I know it sounds strange," she admitted. "But I've done a lot of reading on autism, you know, because of my students. And I began to realize--" She paused again to consider her words. "You see, autism is considered to be a spectrum disorder--I've told you this before--one person may be brilliant, and another person may have severe cognitive impairments--but they may have similar symptoms. At this point the diagnoses are done symptomatically; there's no blood test or genetic marker that proves you have it. So I could never prove that Charlie had Asperger's. It was a gut feeling I had."

Dale nodded, his mouth pressed tight, his eyebrows low. "Why did you think that? What symptoms did he have?"

Samantha clenched her hands together and felt herself shivering. It was scary to be talking about something she'd never said out loud before. "Well, he had a lot of sensory issues. He seemed to be under sensitive in a way. People like that crave sensation--which may be why he was such a dare devil--leaping off bridges into the river, climbing up Half Dome, going out to play a rough game of football with guys half his age when he was 60 years old! He used to come home with cuts and bruises on his cheeks and forehead. 'It's nothing,' he'd say." Samantha stopped to catch her breath, realizing that her words were spilling out rapidly at a frantic pitch. She stared down at her hands. "You know, when we were first together he was working at a pizza parlor, and he used to come home with big red welts on his wrists and forearms because he routinely burnt himself on the ovens." She looked up at Dale, squaring her shoulders and affecting a husky voice. "'Doesn't hurt, Sam,' he'd say. 'If you're going to work with fire, you're going to get burnt.'"

"He used to say that to me too!" Dale exclaimed and he leapt to his feet. "I used to feel like a wussy sometimes compared to him." He headed toward the back of the house, flipping on light switches as he went. Samantha saw him enter a small kitchenette behind a granite counter. He came back with a bowl and a bag of tortilla chips. "God, he was tough as nails!" He filled the bowl and set it on the table before Samantha. He kept the bag for himself, hunkering back down in his chair, taking a big handful of chips and shoving them in his mouth. Samantha tried to hide her smile, but she suspected this was the Dale only Charlie ever saw. She felt honored to get this glimpse. She leaned forward to daintily take a few chips for herself.

"There's more," she said, chewing carefully. She swallowed. "He, uh, well, he liked to sleep wrapped up in that tight mummy sleeping bag of his. He'd rather sleep in that thing than in bed with me sometimes." She bit another chip. "He visited our bed often," she said with a modest shrug, "but he preferred to sleep in the bag. It used to bother me; I felt rejected. But I was reading about this all the time because of my students, and well, I came to understand. Anyway, usually he would sleep on the floor of our bedroom--silly as that sounds--and often he liked to sleep outside in the open air."

Dale nodded, his mouth still full. "He said he liked to sleep under the open sky to open his crown chakra up to the universe."

Samantha shrugged. "Whatever."

Dale laughed. "I thought you were the energetic queen my dad searched for all his adult life. And now you give it a dismissive 'whatever!?'"

"Don't misunderstand me now," Samantha said, smiling at the seeming contradiction. "I am open to all these ideas. Maybe sometimes these physiological issues arise so that our vehicles will be led to search for a solution, and in that way, the spiritual path opens to us. Anything--and everything--is possible. I came to believe--to know--that Charlie had sensory integration issues. I saw them come up too often."

"But is that all there is to Asperger's Syndrome?" Dale asked.

Samantha shook her head. "No, there were other things: first of all, your father was brilliant. He could read faster than anybody I've ever known, and he could add up a long column of numbers in his head. It was remarkable."

"I remember that too," Dale agreed. "I used to think in

school that I was pretty stupid compared to him. I couldn't get through arithmetic the way he did. I asked him to stop helping me with my homework; it made me feel worse afterwards." He stuffed more chips in his mouth and chewed thoughtfully. "So you think that's another symptom?"

"Well, it could be," Samantha continued. She pushed the bowl of chips out of reach to avoid temptation. "He also had a lot of things he would obsess on. All the spiritual stuff is an obvious example." Feeling more relaxed now, she leaned back into the couch. "You know, I like to feel that the universe is leading me where I need to go on my path--but I still go to work in the morning. I still make plans for more than a half hour in advance. That was the hardest part of the relationship--wondering if he'd show up for dinner or if he'd be down by the river or up in the mountains. I got used to making plans for Mariah and me without him. But the older he got, the more often he'd join us." She took a deep breath and stared down at her hands. "I made my peace with it."

"Must have been hard," Dale said sympathetically.

Samantha nodded, blinking rapidly. "It was, I won't gloss it over," she said sadly. "But I wouldn't trade my life with Charlie for all the golden thimbles and dresser sets."

Dale smiled as he tossed the near-empty bag of chips onto the burl wood table. He let his hands hang down below his knees.

Samantha stood. "Guess I'm going to go back to bed." She moved toward the door.

"Sam--?" Dale called her back.

"Hmmm--?"

"That student of yours--Luisa? You said she was autistic, didn't you?"

"Yeah, she is," Samantha replied. "Very severe case, no doubt about her diagnosis."

"I understand," Dale said. "So can I have her email address now?"

"Sure, sweetie; I'll get it for you in the morning."

"No," he said meekly. "Can I have it now? Do you know it?" He began to pat his shirt as if looking for a pen.

"Actually, I think I do remember it, so yeah, I think I can give it to you now if you want," she said.

"Here," he said handing her a pen. "Well--" he said pulling out the nearly empty pack of Camels. "Guess this is the closest thing I have to paper right now."

She shrugged as she accepted the pack. "It'll do."

She jotted on the soft-sided pack then handed it back. Three cigarettes were still inside. He pulled them out and handed them to her. "You want to get rid of these for me, please?"

"My pleasure," she said with a smile.

Chapter Eight

Early the next morning, Geneva took Mariah to a shop in town and bought her a pair of dark brown leather boots. They stretched on like a pair of gloves hugging her foot and ankle. Somehow she felt powerful in these boots, and she was very grateful for them. "As long as you get them re-soled every few years, these boots could last you the rest of your life," Geneva told her.

Mariah smiled, wondering what she would be like in ten, twenty, fifty or even seventy years from now. Would she still be wearing a pair of denim trousers and a cotton shirt with these boots? She sat on a chair in the shop, looking down at the boots, then stretched her legs out to get a different view. She was tempted to tip back and lift her legs in the air, but she resisted that childish urge. There was something about these boots that made her feel womanly. They were not the latest teen fashion; they were timeless classics, and now so was she. She was the woman who would inhabit this body, and these boots, for decades to come. She was Mariah.

They met her mother, brother and aunt in a sandwich shop a half block down the street. They bought their lunch to go, packed it up in their satchels and set out for a hike along Oak Creek to Cathedral Rock. Geneva led them to a well-advertised vortex, fabled to emit a subtle force that could balance the spiritual energy of anyone in close proximity to it. Samantha and Mariah held hands as they took their turn sitting in the cradle of this so-called energy center. Mariah rested her head on her mother's shoulder. "Do you feel different?" she whispered.

Samantha chuckled. "Not really."

"Me neither." Mariah frowned. "Do you think it's a hoax?"

"Oh, no," Samantha said quickly. "I like to think I am always a willing conductor for universal energy. Maybe you and I are already vortices! This is how we always feel: maybe it's impossible for this spot to enhance our energy any more than it already is! We'd be so powerful we'd implode!"

Mariah knew her mother was joking, but she could only nod.

"What are you thinking?" Samantha asked.

"I'm thinking I'm too sad to be a vortex," Mariah said slowly.

Samantha squeezed her hand. "I know," she agreed. "Me too."

***

That evening back at Geneva's house they ate a light dinner of adobo chicken, corn and cactus salad, and mango sherbet for dessert. Later the women sat out on the patio under the desert stars, sipping Sangria, feeling tired and content. "I'm so grateful we had the chance to come out here, Geneva," Samantha said. "Your home is beautiful."

"Yes, thank you, Geneva," Mariah echoed.

"Mmmm, hmmm," Hyacinth murmured, tipping her chaise lounge back a few more inches and gazing up at the sky. "Arizona is beautiful and California is beautiful: and to think I spent so many years resenting the American west."

Mariah sat up a bit straighter in her lounge chair, startled by her aunt's confession.

"What?" Samantha exclaimed. "Did I hear you right? You don't sound resentful."

Hyacinth cleared her throat. "Oh," she said sounding regretful. "You've all been so kind I guess I'm going to have to let that go."

"Let what go?" Samantha persisted in her teacher voice.

Hyacinth swung her lounger back to an upright position. "Well, you see," she began, "California stole my brother away. It's hard when you live in a place that has summer for a week and a half to compete with California! All that blasted sunshine!" She laughed but it sounded forced. Mariah sensed her aunt wasn't joking.

"So you blame California for Charlie leaving New England," Geneva restated in her clipped professorial tone. "Do I understand you correctly?"

Hyacinth laughed again, running her finger around the rim of her glass. "I'm just making a little funny," she said.

Samantha and Geneva both spoke at once "Well, he only came out west because I was accepted at Berkeley, so really--" Geneva began, but Samantha drowned her out. "I guess you could blame me, oh—sorry, Geneva." Both women paused and gestured for the other to continue but Mariah burst in with a passionate plea, silencing them.

"Aunt Hy," she exclaimed, "I'm glad you were angry at California, you know--instead of being angry at me."

"Oh, Mariah," Hyacinth said as she leaned forward to squeeze her niece's hand. "I was angry at you once," she told her. "I nearly had your father talked into moving home. Our mother had had a stroke and wasn't doing well. Dale was a senior in high school. The time was right."

"I remember," Samantha admitted.

"I'm sure you do," Hyacinth agreed. "Yes, I thought he would move home. But then along comes this baby girl. Oh, I was not happy."

"Oh, Hyacinth," Samantha said gently. "I'd say I'm sorry, but I'm sure you wouldn't believe me."

"Oh, no, Samantha, you don't need to apologize! I came out to your wedding and I met you and this charming infant—well, you both won me over. Even Dale and his friends were dancing with you at the wedding, Mariah. Can you believe that?"

"I've seen the photos," Mariah confirmed with a modest smile.

"So I stopped being angry with you," Hyacinth said as she nervously straightened her blouse. "But I've never quite let California off the hook. Pretty, pretty California: so affected, so spoiled with its pretty weather and its world class wine and its movie stars."

Mariah exchanged glances with her mother. She could see that Samantha was amused but speechless.

Geneva rose to re-fill glasses. "You know, Hy," she said as she lifted the pitcher. "I think you made a good choice. If you've got to be angry at somebody you need to pick a worthy adversary. The Pacific Ocean can take it. The Sierra Nevada—those mountains can handle it. The state of California is a lot harder and stronger than some folks give it credit for. And it's got that plush valley too. Trust me, California can take your anger and then welcome you in anyway."

"Ha!" Hyacinth laughed in surprise and lifted her glass to salute Geneva's wisdom. "I've never thought of it that way. I guess you're right, Geneva!"

"She is right," Samantha affirmed, lifting her glass as well.

"Because you are always welcome at our home in California."

"Thank you, Samantha," Hyacinth said in her husky voice. "When Dale said the Easter family has a west coast branch now—well, I was stunned." She shook her head and sipped her wine. "All these years, I'd been thinking of you camping at a foreign outpost. Surely, I thought, I'd reel you back in eventually. But I guess I need to resign myself--"

"Oh, please don't think of it that way," Samantha interrupted. "The world is a lot smaller than it used to be."

"You're right," Hyacinth agreed. "And I hope you'll feel free to visit me at home in New England. It's colder and darker back there, but that side of life is worth a bit of exploring too."

***

Dale was in the guesthouse, typing on his laptop. Luisa had declined his offer of a video chat but she did send a recent photograph that he gazed at as they conversed through the written word.

"It sounds like your father was a fascinating man," Luisa's words appeared on his screen. "I do remember meeting him once about fifteen years ago when I was in my teens. I remember he had endearing crinkles around the corners of his eyes. It was his eyes that made his smile so engaging."

"Oh my God," Dale typed. "Your description brings his face into my mind. I'm blinking back tears, I miss him so much."

As soon as he pushed SEND he drew back in surprise. I can't believe I admitted that to her, he thought. Somehow it felt natural. But maybe he was fooling himself. Maybe it was this medium--the computer--that was making him so bold. He was one step--no, many steps--removed from her. He could imagine she was anything and everything he wanted and needed her to be. He wanted to believe that she was his soul mate, that she would reveal herself willingly to him this way as well, that they could have a connection as easy and natural in person. Yet this was silly. If only he could pull those words back that he had just sent over the wireless space between Arizona and Connecticut. But it was too late.

"There was a professor here at Yale that I was very close to," Luisa's responded. "I suppose in many ways he was a father to me too. He helped teach me to type so I could communicate with you and with everyone else in the world around me. It was very difficult for me when he dropped his body and went on to his next incarnation. So I can understand--in a small way--the pain you are going through as you live now without the physical presence of your father."

Dale shoved a few tortilla chips in his mouth and immediately forgot his earlier apprehension. "What was your professor's name?" he asked. "What kinds of things did you like to do together?"

"His name was Dom, short for Dominic."

"Dominic," Dale whispered as he stared at the screen. He could see she was still typing, so he leaned back in his chair to wait. *I'm smiling,* he realized. *I'm having fun.* He took a deep breath; her reply was coming in now.

"When I first knew him," she said, "we often watched TV shows and movies together. He wanted me to learn about the emotions of my neuro-typical peers, by which I mean people who do not have autism. So we would watch comedies like *I Love Lucy* and we would discuss why it was funny. And we would watch sad movies too--like Romeo and Juliet--so we could discuss why it was sad. My favorite show was *The Mary Tyler Moore Show* because it was funny but it was also about an independent woman who was living life on her own terms. I liked that."

Dale read bits of the conversation aloud as if Luisa was in the room with him. "Mary Tyler Moore! Oh, yeah, I remember." He set his fingers on the keys. "Some of those old shows from the 70s were the best, weren't they?" he typed. "My dad liked to watch the old reruns of *All in the Family*. We really used to laugh at that because it was poking fun at bigots and showing how silly their prejudices are."

"Yes! I remember that one," Luisa wrote. "Archie Bunker liked to label everybody and put them into neat little boxes so they would be easier for him to deal with. People like to do that with those of us who have disabilities too. I love the character of his wife. Oh, what was her name?"

"Edith! She was hilarious," Dale responded. And they typed like this for half the night.

***

Mariah was up before dawn, sitting cross-legged before an eastern window, her notebook computer balanced on her knees. Refrigerator hum, ticking clock, and padding of her fingers on computer keys gave a shape to the silence. She rocked between the screen and the sunrise. A sky streaked salmon pink and gray urged her to use this time for meditation and prayer, but the Facebook and Twitter posts of friends back home were calling her to come out and play. She'd had no contact with home since her father's funeral. She felt interested but detached, as if she had wandered ahead on a path where her teenaged peers could not follow.

She was not ready to respond to their messages. She folded her hands and gazed out the window, watching as red became pink became orange, then finally yellow and blue. She closed her eyes and meditated.

Only then did she allow herself to log onto e-bay. She didn't need to search long. She jumped to her feet, rushed down the hall and burst into the guest room.

Her mother's eyes were still closed, but Mariah bounded onto the bed. "Mom!" she screeched. "Look!"

Samantha was used to a restless partner sharing her bed. She rolled toward her daughter. "What?" she mumbled. Mariah tapped the computer screen and Samantha half sat up, the better to focus.

"Oh, my God," she said in a low keyed but intense tone. "Is that it? Is that the thimble?"

"I'm positive it is," Mariah said. "There's the identifying mark by his eyelid--the tiny lower case e!"

"Go ask Hyacinth," Samantha commanded. "We need to be sure."

"Okay," Mariah shouted joyfully and she cavorted down the staircase. "Auntie Hy," she hollered. "Where are you?"

Samantha stared at the screen. Oh, no. The thimble--if this was indeed the Easter family thimble--was in Minnesota.

***

Dale turned away from Mariah's laptop to sip his coffee. "Minnesota is one long drive, Mariah," he stated in a flat, tired voice.

Geneva set a platter of scrambled eggs and sausage on the table. "You've come this far, Dale," his mother said. "Surely you're not going to jump ship now."

"Mom," he countered, as he grabbed the computer and pounded in a few keystrokes, "it's--whoa--look at that, it's fifteen hundred and eighty—jeez, nearly sixteen hundred miles from Sedona to Victory, Minnesota! This is not your typical evening cruise! This is a long long way!"

Mariah stared at her brother over her empty plate, feeling too excited to eat. "Oh, Dale, it would be fun."

Hyacinth paused as she spread green pepper jelly on her toast. "I would love to go, Mariah, but I've got a fundraiser next week in New Haven. But, Dale, if you need to get home, I'm happy to buy you a plane ticket. Too bad we can't take the same plane, but we could share a cab to the airport."

"Thanks, Aunt Hy," Dale said. "I appreciate the offer but I'm not ready to fly off yet."

"So you'll come with us!" Mariah squealed.

"Hold on, Mare; let's take a deep breath or two." He spoke in a voice that seemed deliberately slow. "I think we should all head back to our respective coasts and you know, reassess. I need to get back to work--and Samantha--both you and Mariah have classrooms that are waiting for you."

Samantha held her coffee mug near her chest with both hands like a shield. "If Mariah wants to drive to Minnesota," she said decisively, "I'm game."

"Yes!" Mariah cried, but the other women were silent with expectation, glancing between Dale and Samantha, wondering if a showdown might be immanent. Stepmother and son stared at each other for a long moment, then glanced away. "More coffee?" Geneva asked, standing to retrieve the pot.

Hyacinth leaned toward Samantha. "I'll bet you're not ready to go back to a house without Charlie in it, huh?"

Samantha was stunned at the question. She noted that Dale had lifted his head to turn to her. She glanced down at her hands and nodded. "Yeah, I guess that's a big part of it; I shouldn't be ashamed to admit that. As long as I'm out here away from home, I don't have to face reality. If there is such a thing as reality."

Mariah nodded. "Daddy used to say that this so-called reality was God dreaming she was seven billion people."

Geneva laughed. "I remember him saying that over forty years ago. I always liked that."

"Well, there may be something to it," Dale said, and everyone turned to look at him in surprise.

"What?" he asked with a defensive shrug.

"Nothing," Samantha spoke for all of them, though she couldn't help smiling.

"Dale looks like he's in love again," Mariah said slyly.

Dale swung around in his chair to gape at her. "Why do you say that?"

"I don't know," she said defensively. "I was just teasing, I guess. It came to me." Her voice trailed off, hoping he would supply some hidden information, but he turned back to his computer screen with an annoyed sigh.

"I want you to come with us," Samantha said in her directive teacher voice and again all eyes turned to Dale. He said nothing, continuing to tap on his computer keys.

"What are you doing?" Geneva asked as she came to look over his shoulder.

"Just a sec," he said sharply, then he looked up. "Okay, so we head east to Oklahoma, then turn north—"

"Wouldn't it be prettier to head up to Colorado, then head east when we get to, oh, maybe South Dakota?" Samantha asked.

"A lovely route is up along the Mississippi through Kansas and Iowa," Geneva told her.

Mariah threw herself into Dale's lap. "I knew you wouldn't desert us!"

"First things first," Dale announced, his attention still trained on the screen, "Let's negotiate a good deal with this vendor--and make sure this guy knows how to lock up his merchandise for safe keeping."

Chapter Nine

On the road, Mariah sat in the back seat watching the scenery change from desert to mountains. "Do either of you know anybody in Minnesota?" she asked.

"No," Dale said quickly. "You, Sam?"

"No."

"Not much synchronicity this time, huh?" Dale said, and as soon as the words were out of his mouth he wanted to pull them back in, hoping he hadn't sounded too smug.

"It certainly doesn't appear that way," Samantha said, "but appearances can be illusory."

"In the eye of the beholder," Dale quoted.

"Something like that," Samantha acknowledged.

They drove silently for a few miles, the road curving and climbing. Finally the asphalt evened out and traffic thinned. Dale took a swig of water from a bottle perched near the gearshift. He cleared his throat. "Luisa seems very spiritual," he announced suddenly.

"You know Luisa?" Mariah asked.

"We've been emailing," Dale said in a voice deliberately casual.

"I love to email with Luisa," Mariah said. "Though I don't do it very often. She's very busy, and I've got so much school work, and you know you get out of a habit--but gee whiz--why am I babbling about all this--Dale!--You're corresponding with Luisa! That is so cool!"

Dale's fingers fidgeted on the steering wheel. "Yeah," he said with a grin. "It is cool."

Samantha couldn't hide her own smile as she leaned back in the passenger seat. "Luisa's told you, hasn't she?--that she's a professor in the Comparative Religions Department at Yale?"

"She's a professor--? Where? Comparative Religions? You're kidding."

"She didn't tell you that?" Mariah said incredulous. "What did you talk about?"

Dale shifted down as the road wound upward. "Well, we talked about old TV shows and movies. Books. Our favorite bodies of water--"

"Bodies of water?" Mariah repeated.

"Yeah." He chuckled, seeming a little proud of the novelty of their conversation. "We had a long discussion comparing Atlantic and Pacific beaches. Luisa loves to swim. Oh, she told me she loved swimming in Walden Pond."

"Walden Pond? You mean where Henry David Thoreau lived?" Mariah exclaimed. "I remember going to Walden Pond. I was really little."

"You were only three," Samantha told her.

"I still remember it."

"Okay."

Mariah sighed. "Daddy loved Walden Pond."

"Yeah, he did," Samantha agreed softly.

They fell into a deep silence as the road dipped and twisted. Samantha felt guilty that she was allowing her own sadness to radiate through the car. Finally Dale spoke.

"We did spend a lot of time talking about Dad," he revealed. "And about our parents in general. She wrote a lot about her mom--your friend who owns the string of pie shops, Sam. She sounds like a very strong personality."

"That she is!" Samantha confirmed. "Anna decides what she wants and she goes for it. Years ago, she offered me a lot of money to go back to Connecticut to work with her. I said no, and she just hounded me." Samantha reached into her tote for her own bottle of water. "When she could see that I wouldn't leave California, she insisted I sign on as a paid consultant. She paid me for video chats and phone calls and such. I told her I'd do it for free, but she said no, she liked the sense of power it gave her to make me her employee. And she owned right up to that—'I like the power,' she said. I was floored at her candor." She took a sip of liquid. "I guess we all like a little bit of power sometimes."

"I don't think I'd like power," Mariah said crinkling her nose.

"But you want autonomy, don't you?" her mother asked. "You like to be able to make your own decisions, go where you want to go, do what you want to do?"

"Well, sure, but I don't want to have power over other people," she said. "It doesn't sound very nice." Her voice sounded humble, almost diminutive.

"That's a good attitude, Mare," Dale encouraged her. "I hope you'll always stay true to that sweetness at your core."

Mariah twisted her mouth at her brother's words. "Yeah," she said with an uncertain lilt.

Samantha watched her daughter's reaction. Sweetness at the core, Samantha thought. Something like that seldom lasted. It wasn't meant to.

"You know," Samantha said, "Luisa has a pretty strong personality herself. Does she appreciate her mother's strength or has that created a barrier between them?" She lowered her chin. "If you don't mind my asking."

Dale took another sip from his water bottle. "Well, I don't mean to break confidences," he said, "but I think Luisa would say that both are true. She said her mother had come from a working class background without much money, but she became a multi-millionaire mainly through her creativity and her determination to work hard. Of course Luisa admires that. But she also admits she herself has a strong will and at times they've knocked heads."

"I only ask because, well, I wonder. . ." Samantha let her voice trail off, afraid to say that she was concerned that someday Mariah would become as opinionated as she herself was. She wanted Mariah to be strong, but what happened to mother /daughter relationships then? Many don't survive, that seemed likely. She looked back at Mariah, staring out the window as they passed goats and cows grazing in the mountain meadows. Samantha felt her heart swell.

"But Dale," Mariah jumped in, "even though Luisa didn't tell you which department she teaches in, you did get a sense of her spirituality, didn't you?"

"Oh definitely," Dale agreed. "She has this sense of--I guess you'd call it destiny. It's not so much that she thinks everything is planned out ahead of time, but well--" He paused, seeming to struggle for the right words. He looked at Samantha, and she wondered if he was seeking help in articulating these new ideas. But she was determined to stay in patient-teacher-mode, waiting for Dale to say it himself. "Well," he said finally with a seemingly embarrassed laugh, "she talks a lot about Divine Energy." He glanced again at his stepmother, even took a peek in the rear view mirror at his sister, perhaps expecting them to tease him that he was finally finally embracing these concepts. But they only smiled knowingly at each other and at him. "Yeah," he said again, "energy. Divine Energy, a consciousness, she said, that wants nothing more than to reveal itself to us And here we are subsumed by it, and yet unaware."

"Yeah," Samantha murmured in a trance-like voice.

He laughed. "So I got that right?"

"There's no right or wrong here," Samantha assured him.

"I guess," he continued. "Luisa told me she feels we are all of us weaving energetic webs. Like blue prints--for the enlightenment of the planet."

"Yes, exactly," Samantha said.

"So you believe that too?" Dale asked.

"It's what I like to believe," she nodded. "I have enough doubt that I don't speak in absolutes the way Luisa does. But your father accepted her precepts. He loved to read her articles."

"She's published articles?" Dale asked.

"In some academic journals, but also in a literary journal called The Sun, and a popular Buddhist journal called Tricycle. She's been quite prolific."

"She didn't mention anything about that," he noted.

"Sounds like you two had a conversation that was different than the ones she typically has," Mariah said.

Dale tried to disguise his smile. "Maybe," he said shyly.

***

During this leg of the journey, without Hyacinth, the family was more subdued. They watched the road and the passing scenery in comfortable silence, as only those who have known and cared for each other a long time can do. Mariah found an app to identify wild flowers and birds and spent a lot of time shifting her gaze from her phone through the window and back again. Samantha spent many hours stretched out on the back seat sound asleep.

"I hope Mom is okay," Mariah whispered to Dale on the second afternoon. "She's been asleep a long time."

"She's grieving, Mare," Dale said. "It's draining, you know, to feel that much emotion."

Mariah turned off her phone and stared at the white line on the road before them. After a long silence she turned again to her brother. "Dale," she said, "let me drive."

He took a quick glance at his baby sister, then shifted his eyes back to the road. He knew the terrain ahead was relatively flat. It would be a good training ground for her—and for himself as well. "Okay," he agreed, and he pulled over right then and there.

Samantha didn't even wake up.

***

After six days of brother and sister sharing the wheel, they arrived in Victory. As they drove into the city center, their Map Quest print-outs seemed useless. "This place is like a Skinner box," Dale complained as he tried to navigate around the tiny patchwork quilt of a town. "Can you tell, Mariah?--are we headed north or south now?"

"From the map I'd say we were heading west," Mariah said tentatively. "But the sun is behind us so we must be going east."

"Maybe we've reached one of those mysterious places on the globe where the ordinary rules of magnetism don't apply," Dale joked. "You know, like at the north pole, do the compasses point straight up in the air? Whatever direction you step in, you've got to be heading south, right?"

"So you think maybe every direction here is east? Or is it west?" Mariah asked.

Samantha leaned forward from her perch in the back seat. "I don't know which way we're going," she said. "But I need a hamburger. Can we make that happen?"

"I haven't seen any McDonald's or Burger Kings," Dale said.

"And I hope we don't," Samantha retorted. "This is a small town; there's got to be a good diner or coffee shop around here someplace."

"There's a Taco Bell ahead," Mariah said pointing.

"Oh, no," Dale and Samantha said in near unison.

"Sweetie, if you learn nothing else from this trip," her mother said with mock pedantry, "never eat Mexican food this far from Mexico. I don't care if it is a Taco Bell."

"I ate at a Mexican restaurant in Canada once," Dale confessed. "Big mistake. That Irish mashed potato and cauliflower dish you make, Sam--even that is spicier!"

Mariah sighed, a little impatient that they were lecturing her on the virtues of choosing the right fast food restaurant as if she were a kid or something. She studied the map as her mother and brother laughed about the relative seasonings of various dining options available at family dinners on Thanksgiving and Christmas, the bland Irish fare favored by too many of Samantha's cousins, contrasted with the wonderfully vinegary German potato salad recipe handed down from Charlie's mother. For heat nothing could rival the green salsa offered at that delicious dive on Broadway a few blocks from Samantha's and Charlie's house.

"Oh, look," Mariah cried suddenly as they passed a particularly seedy block of buildings edged with weedy lawns and cracked pavement.

"A burger joint?" Samantha asked.

"No, no," Mariah pleaded. "Slow down, I think we're getting really close to that Antique Row where the vendor said his shop is. Yeah--turn right at the next light--it should be Madison. There it is--that's it, turn right."

Dale obeyed, leading them to a narrow curvy road darkened by the shade of dozens and dozens of leafy oak trees that stretched across the asphalt. "It's down here," Mariah cried again. "Turn left into this lot."

"Antique Row," read a shingle that hung from a post at the entryway. The lot was lined with shops, some more attractive than others. "What's the name again?" Dale asked.

"The White House," Mariah read off the slip she held in her hand. "I don't see it." A trace of anxiety tinged her voice.

"Sit tight, Mare," Dale assured her. "This lot is bigger than it looks."

The parking lot took another sharp twist and they could see now that it dead-ended at the back of a levee. There at the end was a tiny white washed shack with a flat roof covered with brown and withered wisteria vines. "Seems our train has come into the terminal," Dale announced as if he were a conductor. "Welcome to your destination."

"Looks kind of creepy," Mariah said cautiously.

"And yet we soldier bravely on," her mother said with mock bravado. "Remember! We're on a quest."

Mariah nodded quietly. "We're on a quest," she whispered to herself to strengthen her resolve.

Dale was already ahead of them, trying the doorknob. "It's locked!" he said in dismay.

"It's past five o'clock," Samantha noted with a sigh. "Maybe it's closed."

"It's Saturday night," Dale said, and their sign here says they're open till six on Saturdays." He began to thump loudly on the door, bending down to peek through the windows. "Here comes somebody," Dale said, satisfied.

The man who opened the door a crack was short and stout with multiple chins. He was shaped like a keg of beer, carrying most of his weight around his chest and neck. "What's your problem, man?" he bit off the words in his gruff but high-pitched voice. "Can't you see we're closed?"

"No, I couldn't see that," Dale said. "Especially since it says you're open till six."

"And it's six fifteen, college boy! Now get your ass off my porch!"

"Oh, Dale," Samantha said suddenly, "it is after six. We changed time zones! I forgot!"

"Good for you, lady; honest mistake. That's just great. Now go away!"

Samantha and Dale stood struck by the man's ornery demeanor, but Mariah stepped up. "Sir, we've come to make a $600 purchase."

The man turned toward Mariah and licked his lips. "Okay, now you're talking. But as they say in Tom Cruise movies, show me the money."

"I've already sent you my credit card number," Samantha

said, her impatience apparent. "All we want is to pick up the gold thimble. We've nearly completed the transaction online. So give us our thimble, and we'll be on our way."

"You gave him your credit card number?" Dale said in a scolding voice. "What were you thinking?"

The man snorted, interrupting them. "I knew you people were wasting my time! That thimble was stolen this morning. When I came in, it had vanished, okay? Gone with the wind! So as nice as your story sounds, I got no business with you."

"No!" Mariah cried. "This can't be happening again." Her eyes began to tear up and Shorty gave her a look of disgust.

"Whatever, girly. Go get weepy someplace else, I ain't got the time."

Dale pushed forward against the door, planting his foot inside. "Well, you better make the time, mister! You either get us the thimble, or we're coming in so we can see you cancel my stepmother's credit card purchase. Now what's it going to be?"

"I told you I ain't got the thimble," the little man shouted.

Dale pulled out his wallet and carefully removed a business card toting the fact that he was a lawyer not to be messed with. "You better let us in or I'll be calling your police department. Of course, that's nothing compared to what I'll do once I get you in court. I'll sue you for all you're worth. Although this White House here is obviously not worth the time of day. Still I'd do it for fun."

Mariah's eyes grew wide listening to her brother trash talk the little man. The man stepped aside and waved them through the narrow doorway. The light was dim inside, and Mariah took her mother's arm.

The ceiling seemed unusually low and the place was filled with old and cheap looking knickknacks and dusty frayed furniture. "Did you ever even have this thimble?" Dale said accusingly. "This doesn't seem to be the kind of business that deals in fine collectables like my family's thimble."

"Of course I had it," the little man whined. "See it came in this box."

He pulled a tiny lavender colored box off a shelf and Mariah gasped. "Mom! That's the box Aunt Hy put the thimble in for me!"

"You're right, Mariah!" Samantha exclaimed. "Dale, he did have it. He did!"

Dale fingered the white tissue paper inside the box. "How do we know you don't still have it?"

The man snorted. "You people drove here from California or wherever the hell you came from!--and you're willing to give me your credit card number, shit--nobody wants that thing more than you do. Why wouldn't I give it to ya? Nobody else is going to pay me half as much."

"Get my credit card info and let's get out of here, Dale," Samantha said in a soft voice. "This place makes me sad."

"You're going to have to close your account," Dale said with a deep breath of surrender. "But if this purchase has already gone through," he continued, turning a threatening finger to the little man, "the police will hear about it."

"Well of course the purchase has already gone through!" the man exclaimed in a whiny defensive voice. "I had the thimble and I had every intention of handing it over to you. But it got stolen! What part of that don't you understand?"

"And what part of this don't you understand," Dale countered. "Cancel the charge. Right now. Tonight. Or the police will be notified."

"Of course I'll cancel it!" He hastened to a phone near a

computer and fax machine. The Easters waited silently as he made a call. Mariah stood frozen, staring at but not really seeing the dusty tchotchkes that packed the shelves around her. She felt angry at this little man, angry at life, and angry at herself. She was sinking into a hole, here on this sallow linoleum. She hated her own passivity. But what could she do? She looked at her mother, exhausted, leaning on a counter crowded with old Pez dispensers and well-worn plastic action figures. Dale was yawning and stretching. The fax machine hummed on and the little man handed over a receipt to her brother. Dale didn't even thank him. "Let's get out of here," he muttered, wrapping a protective arm around Samantha.

"Wait," Mariah said, realizing there was at least one small thing she could do for her family. "Before we leave, sir," she said sweetly, "could you tell us how to get to the other side of the river?" She indicated the map she still held in her hand. "We have a reservation at a hotel and I think it's over there."

"Well, you're going to be late for your reservation, sweetheart, because the only way over this river is miles from here. Way off your map."

"But there's a bridge right here," Mariah pleaded, pointing on her map.

"That bridge has been out for months," the man said dismissively. "You're plain out of luck."

Chapter Ten

They found a Denny's a few blocks over that was clean and well lit. Across its parking lot was a Motel 6 and Samantha suggested they cancel their reservation at the nicer hotel and just stay. "I'm so tired," she said, yawning. "I forgot I'm not a spring chicken anymore."

Dale and Mariah quickly agreed to the accommodations, but when they went inside to the registration desk, they found there was only one vacant room.

"I'll sleep in the van," Dale offered.

"Don't be silly," Samantha said. "We're family for goodness sake. There'll be two double beds; Mariah and I will take one and you'll take the other. This isn't a problem."

Dale nodded quietly. Mariah could see that her mother and half brother were both very tired and she felt responsible. She had dragged them nearly as far south as you could go without hitting Mexico, then as far north as you could go without crossing into Canada. And for what? Nothing--a thimble, a tiny little gold thimble. What did it mean anyway? Something to do with hawks: hawks probably glare down at people on the street all the time. Why wouldn't they? They're predators; they have keen eyesight--her father had said so. Of course a predator is going to be smart enough to watch out for even bigger predators, and there's nobody bigger than predators of the human variety. So they're going to watch, they're going to look: what's unusual is that Mariah had looked back.

What's more, just because there were two hawks on the thimble, she had gone and invented some strange fantasy that the universe was sending her a message about her twin. And what was this business about a twin anyway? So there had been another fertilized egg floating around inside her mother the same time Mariah's own little ovum floated down to her mother's uterus. So what? Maybe that egg was just an egg, not a person, not a soul, a bit of flotsam and jetsam that got stuck in a tube and lost. Maybe there was no person there; no entity that intended to incarnate. That would have been very bad planning, now wouldn't it? She was the only spirit that made this trip and incarnated through the love of Samantha and Charlie Easter. It was silly of her to come up with such an elaborate fantasy, especially when they were all mourning her father's passing. What a burden she'd placed on her family, making them come so far. They would all look back at this and think of her as crazy. Maybe they would laugh, maybe they would remember it fondly—"Yes, Mariah, you gave us a little scare there with your strange obsession with this thimble. Admittedly we needed the distraction, but thank God you snapped out of it."

And snap out of it she would. We'll head back to California, she told herself, and I'll be a model student from now on. I'll finish high school, I'll go on to college and everyone will say I am a credit to my parents.

Or maybe, she thought, I'll end up in some state institution, babbling and crying all the time. Everyone will look back at this trip as the turning point. Her mother and brother will shake their heads and dab at their wet eyes. "Why didn't we realize?" they'll ask futilely. "Maybe we could have done something if we'd realized sooner how crazy she was. But we wanted to believe in something magical too. We all missed Charlie Easter. He was magic and we wanted to believe his daughter had a bit of that gift. But she was sad and crazy. Why didn't we see?"

***

Mariah could hear her brother snoring and her mother's even breath wheezing softly. They were fast asleep. She crept out of bed, pulled on her jeans and her boots, grabbed her backpack and tiptoed out the door.

She didn't know where she was going. She only knew she had to walk off all the sadness that was soaking her limbs. The road was dotted with neon signs, motels and fast food restaurants. She rounded the corner and saw a little diner called Lulu's with a big blue neon sign that read "Pie." She knew someone named Lulu, and her mother ran a national chain of pie shops. This obviously wasn't one of them, but still Mariah took it as a welcoming sign, an omen. She approached slowly, thinking that perhaps this was the time to give up the search for omens, though she had hardly sought this one. Still, maybe it would be a good time to reject even the omens that fell into her path unbidden. Nonetheless, Lulu's was just two doors down. It seemed inevitable she would enter. Omen or no, it was where the path led.

A bell rang as she pushed the glass door open. The shop looked clean, uncluttered and deserted. She stepped inside and looked about. Was this a mistake? Perhaps the lights and the "open" sign had been left by a careless employee too tired to remember their duty to close shop. Maybe she should leave. But then she heard a low sweet humming, a woman's voice wordlessly singing a hymn of some kind. It started out low, but now it was growing and Mariah thought she recognized the sacred tune. She stood frozen listening, listening. And then the voice burst out, loud with the clarity of a crystal vase. "Ah-vay Ma-ree-e-ah!"

Mariah stood stock still for a moment, afraid to break the spell, letting the majestic voice pour the beloved words over her.

Ave Maria gratia plena,
Maria gratia plena,
Maria gratia plena,
Ave ave Dominus,
Dominus tecum.

Slowly and softly, Mariah began to follow the sound of the full and precious voice. She crept behind the counter, finally pushing open a swinging wooden door with a porthole styled window on it. There on her knees scrubbing the floor with a huge yellow sponge was a big boned woman with blonde, nearly white hair. Unaware of Mariah's presence she sang on:

Nunc et in hora mortis,
In hora mortis nostrae.
In hora, hora mortis nostrae
In hora mortis nostrae,
Ave Maria.

The kitchen was a very small place to contain such a big melodious sound. When she stopped singing the room seemed to shrink in on Mariah as if she was looking through a fish eye lens. Her ears rang with the sudden silence, interrupted by the slight splashing and slopping of the soaked sponge hitting the concrete floor. The walls vibrated with the tiniest noises, the ticking of a clock, the hum of a hot oven. Mariah looked around as if the woman wasn't there, feeling as if she herself was invisible.

"Oh!" the woman cried suddenly, apparently startled as she caught sight of Mariah. "You gave me a start, dear." She rose slowly from her knees, dropping the sponge back into a yellow bucket. "Can I get you something?" she asked. "If you go on back through that door, I can get you a menu. We've got most items available though we're not serving the dinner entrees. I can get you a sandwich though if you like."

Mariah stood staring at the woman, barely believing her ears as the woman transformed from a magnificent angel crouched in benediction into someone ordinary with an ordinary voice. She was very tall and sturdy in a pale yellow waitress uniform and a pair of ugly off-white crepe soled shoes. She wore a small silver acorn on a chain around her neck. Mariah wondered at this place, amazed at how plain and nondescript it was, small yet big enough to contain the voice. Maybe this woman was indeed an angel in disguise, Gabriel or Rafael, perhaps?

"Are you all right?" the woman asked her. "You look a little pale. You must need a bite right away, am I right? Maybe a grilled cheese?"

The woman was less than an arms length away now, and Mariah could see that she towered over her by more than a head. She was probably taller than her brother. She wore a plastic nameplate over her breast pocket that read "Cherry." Cherry was pointing out to the public area, and Mariah's brain and feet finally combined to move her to the other room. "I'm sorry;" Mariah began. "I didn't mean to bother you."

Cherry laughed and the pleasing notes of her sopranic laughter brought back the full richness of her singing voice. "No bother, dear," she said. "It's what I'm here for."

Mariah finally moved from the kitchen to the restaurant area and sat down at the nearest counter stool. "I only wanted a piece of pie," she said meekly, in awe of this angel.

"Oh that's our specialty," Cherry said proudly. "We have chocolate cream, banana cream and coconut cream, cherry, berry, peach and a lovely apricot. We've also got our Minnesota style cheesecake. It's not as rich as a New York style, but our cheese is fresher."

"I've never been to New York," Mariah confessed, "so their cheese cake doesn't impress me."

"Oh," Cherry said with a quick tilt of her head. "Something made me think you were here from a big city. Don't know why." She stared at Mariah. "Don't know why," she said again. "So would it be the cheese cake you'll be having?"

"No," said Mariah. "Not tonight. May I ask--are all the pies made with fresh fruit?"

"Oh, some of the fruit has been frozen, but it's still tasty," Cherry assured her. "We did just get some early blackberries, so the berry pie is very fresh."

"Then I'll have the berry pie," Mariah said decisively.

"Oh, there's a girl that knows her own mind," Cherry said, as she moved behind the counter to get a pie from the display case. "Is this your favorite?" she asked as she plated a slice.

"I'm not sure I have a favorite," Mariah told her. "But once a long time ago, a friend of my mother's made us some berry pie, and I've always remembered how good it was."

"Ice cream?" Cherry asked.

"Yes, please."

Cherry set the pie before her and watched as Mariah took a bite. "Is it as good as your mother's friend's recipe?"

"It's different, but just as good in its way."

"I'm glad," Cherry said.

She stepped away to replace the pie, then Cherry stood back, arms akimbo, considering her customer.

"You know, dear, I see now why I thought you were from a big city: it's those lovely boots you're wearing. Very stylish. We don't see those kind around here."

Mariah swallowed a mouthful of sweet berries and ice cream, and looked down to consider her own footwear. "Thank you," she said. "My brother's mother bought these for me. Well, we bartered for them, and I think I got a good trade."

"Your brother's mother?" Cherry asked with a curious smile. "But isn't the mother of your brother your mother too? Sounds like a very strange riddle."

"Oh, no, he's my half brother," Mariah told her. "We have the same father, but we have different mothers. I just met his mother for the first time last week."

"Ah," Cherry said tipping back her head to show off her long neck. "That makes sense." She picked up a cloth and began to polish the Formica counter top. "It's interesting, isn't it, the connections that DNA will forge among us. Even though your half brother's mother is no blood relation of yours, she feels a connection with you because there is someone you love whom you both share DNA with."

"DNA," Mariah mused. "I guess that would be the connection."

"It's what connects all of us," Cherry told her. "It is the very core that houses the divine spark within each of us. Do not underestimate the pull it has, the magnetism of it."

"What do you mean?"

"It's like a tiny blueprint impressed in each cell of our bodies," Cherry continued in an ethereal tone. "It's the spiritual code that leads us where we need to go. It brought our ancestors here to this continent nearly a millennium ago, and it's pulling you away from your big city here to this little town, to learn to find the path you need to tread, to complete your journey."

Mariah heard the fork in her hand tapping against the side of her plate in the sudden silence. Speechless, she gaped at Cherry. "Cherry," she asked slowly. "How did you know--I mean, why do you say I'm on a journey?"

"Oh, well, it's obvious isn't it?" She pulled at her washcloth, wringing it in her hand. She took a step forward. "So have you seen the Rune stone yet?"

Mariah swallowed a mouthful of pie that still needed a bit of chewing. She sipped from her water glass to recover. "A Rune stone?" she asked, a little embarrassed to admit her ignorance. "I don't know what that is."

"No? Well, what most people come to town to see is the Rune stone. It was found over a hundred years ago, but it's centuries old. You see, a farmer and his son were clearing a field, not so far from here, and they were having a time uprooting an aspen tree. When they finally dug it up, they saw a hulking stone tangled in its roots. All kinds of anthropologists and archeologists have studied it over the decades, and they're still arguing if it's authentic or not! But if you ask me, there's no question it was left here by our Norse ancestors--the Swedes and Norwegians both--to let us know of the struggles they were going through to reach a new land and a new life."

"But what is a Rune stone?" Mariah asked.

"A Rune stone is a tall majestic looking rock. The Norse and the Celtic people used to put them up, you know, like monuments--carved with their own Runic language. They were usually a remembrance of some special event or a tribute to the dead."

"And there's one here in town?"

"That's right. Here in the meadows of Minnesota a ship captain left a record of their failed expedition."

"What does it say?" Mariah asked.

"It says that a crew of Swedes and Norwegians started out together to make a voyage that began in New York State. They came up through the canals that brought them up to the Great Lakes, you know, Huron and Superior. But when they arrived half the crew was dead with blood in their mouths. The historians think it may be they'd brought the Black Plague with them from Europe--which is ironic since it was often the Black Plague they were trying to escape."

"How awful," Mariah said.

"It points to the importance of sacrifice, and following your heart despite the risk."

Mariah nodded thoughtfully. "And people come from all over to get a look at this Rune stone?"

"Well, you won't hear this from anyone else, but it's the stone that draws them here. A granite stone like that, carved with an ancient language--it emits a sacred vibration that lures people in. It wants to be touched."

"Can you touch it?" Mariah asked eagerly. "I mean, do they let you?"

"No, not anymore," Cherry said, "but that's okay. You can't hear the vibrations, you can't touch the granite face, but being in the presence of sacred writing is sometimes enough."

Mariah cocked her head. "Is this Rune stone really that special?" she asked. "You're making it sound mystical-- even magical!"

"It might be. It's not for me to say." She paused. "One thing that's unusual about this stone is that it contains both Runic words and Latin! So surprising! This is one reason why some archeologists try to debunk it. They say--how can this be? Two languages on one stone."

Mariah smiled. "Maybe it's like Spanglish."

Cherry raised her eyebrows. "Spanglish?"

"A combination of English and Spanish," Mariah told her. "It's pretty common in southern California."

"Ah!" Cherry exclaimed. "You're a clever girl! When people are speaking in the vernacular of their own day, there will be an amazing mixture of words, phrases and idioms from neighboring cultures. Why wouldn't there be? There might even be misspellings and grammatical errors. It's only when someone is trying to produce a fraudulent text book example of a particular culture's language that it would be perfect!"

"So what does it say in Latin? Was it something that couldn't be translated into their own Rune language? Is that why the Latin was in there?"

"You have the most interesting questions, dear! And in fact, you're probably right, though no one can know for sure."

"So what was it?" Mariah asked again. "What were the Latin words?"

Cherry smiled. "Ave Maria."

Mariah's mouth dropped open. "Ave Maria?" she repeated in surprise.

"'Ave Maria: Save us from peril,'" Cherry quoted. "It was a prayer said at the funeral of plague victims. But it's a prayer on the lips of any one of us with a lick of sense these days, don't you know."

Mariah was silent for a long moment, afraid she might burst into tears. "I liked listening to you sing," she said finally. "When I was little, a woman sang 'Ave Maria' at my great aunt's funeral. My mother loves it. She's very devoted to Mary, and the song is about Mary, isn't it?"

"Yes, of course; it's the Hail Mary prayer sung in Latin," Cherry informed her.

"Oh, of course it is," Mariah said, remembering something that had been forgotten. "My mother likes to pray the rosary, she says a decade every day. She says it's a very powerful

Red-Tailed Hawk

prayer."

"Your mother is a very wise woman," Cherry said. "Can I get you something more to eat? Do you want to look at our menu?"

"No, thank you," Mariah said. "Cherry, where is this Rune stone? Where would I go to see it?"

"Well it's in a museum just the other side of the river," Cherry said, pointing.

"Oh," Mariah said feeling a little disappointed as she remembered that the bridge was out. "But how do you get across the river? It's a long way to find a bridge, isn't it?"

"Oh, no, dear, the bridge is two blocks over here," she said, continuing to point. "You go up this street and turn left. It will lead you right up to the bridge."

"But the bridge is out," Mariah explained. "This man we met at the antique shop told us that the bridge had been out for months and the city didn't have the money to repair it."

"Oh, my Lord," Cherry exclaimed, "what a wicked lie he told you. There's nothing wrong with the bridge, never has been. How very strange he would tell such a monstrous story."

Mariah felt a sudden burst of adrenaline in her solar plexus. "There's nothing wrong with the bridge? But I don't understand! Why would someone do something like that?"

Cherry shrugged. "He was playing the role he's been assigned in life's little drama, dear. Don't attach to it."

Mariah leaned back on the stool, shocked again at this response. "Maybe he was just an angry person," she said in an uncertain tone. "He seemed to have a hard life, maybe he was very angry and he wanted to take it out on someone else."

"Sound like he was a very bad man," Cherry announced,

then she paused to stare at Mariah. "Why don't you ask the question you really want to ask?"

"What--?"

"Say what you're really thinking!" Cherry commanded.

Mariah sat up and straightened her shoulders. "I guess I'm wondering if there's evil in the world," she said rocking her whole body in a steady nod. "I'm wondering why bad things happen to good people, and why an angry little man wants to hurt people--just to hurt them! I mean if he tried to steal our money, I can understand that. But to be so mean--why would someone do that. Is he evil?"

"Those are good questions," Cherry agreed. "It takes a lot of courage to ask these questions, and it takes a lot of courage to seek the answers."

Mariah toyed with her water glass, staring at the shifting liquid, suddenly too shy to look at the waitress's face.

"Is that what you're seeking?" Cherry's question pierced the silence. "Are you seeking answers? Or is there something else?"

Mariah smiled sadly. "I was seeking something that had been stolen--a little golden thimble," she confessed. "It all seems silly now."

"A quest is never silly," Cherry told her. "Unless the seeker doesn't take it seriously." She paused for a moment but Mariah didn't speak. "Maybe it's not the thimble that's so important. Maybe it's the search, the journey. It's going to lead you someplace else perhaps. That's what makes a quest so exciting; you never know what adventure you'll find along the way!"

Mariah suddenly felt impatient sitting on the stool, as if she couldn't wait to get up and go searching again. "How much was the pie?" she asked.

"Two ninety-five."

Mariah hoisted up her backpack on to the stool and unzipped the top compartment. She pulled out a light jacket she'd stuffed on top and wrapped it round her waist. Next was a large cosmetic case that needed dropping on the counter. The crystal apple popped up, and a bottle of hand lotion. Finally she could see her wallet.

"What treasures you travel with!" Cherry exclaimed as she reached out to gently cup the apple in her palm. "How beautiful this is! But didn't you tell me that you've never been to New York?"

"No, I never have," Mariah confirmed. "This was another gift from my aunt from the east coast. Her mother--my paternal grandmother--she loved New York City, so she wanted me to have this apple."

"It's very beautiful," Cherry said again.

Mariah looked up at Cherry's face and could see that she was enthralled. She almost felt she should offer her the apple, but she didn't want to give it up. "I would not want to part with an apple like this," Cherry said suddenly, and Mariah felt again the stab of adrenaline as if somehow Cherry had gotten inside her head, reading her thoughts before she could even think them. "But perhaps," Cherry continued. "I might have something you'll be needing."

Mariah set four dollars on the counter, then began to reload her backpack, yet leaving the apple set before them. She eyed Cherry cautiously. "Go on," she said in a cool voice, ready to negotiate.

Cherry raised an index finger, signaling her to wait. She came out from behind the counter and strode to a row of coat hooks in the back corner. She pulled out a wool and suede hat.

Mariah had seen hats like these in catalogs from Ireland. "This hat," Cherry said in an animated cable TV sales girl voice, "will keep you warm and dry when you're walking through a storm." She began to hum, *When you walk through a storm.*

Mariah shook her head. "No deal," she said with a dismissive wave of her hand.

"I can offer you some gloves to go with the hat," Cherry said. "You have no idea where this journey of yours will take you, or even how long. You will be happy to be prepared with a warm hat and sturdy gloves."

"What's that in the corner?" Mariah asked, indicating a long stretch of teal colored material.

"That's a cloak," Cherry said defensively. "I doubt you'd be interested in it."

Mariah smiled. "It must be a special cloak," she said. "But is it as special as my crystal apple?"

"It might be," Cherry conceded.

"May I see it?"

Cherry lifted the long cloak off her hook and brought it toward Mariah as if carrying a platter of holiday food.

"It's such a beautiful color," Mariah said. "I've always loved this color. And the material is so soft."

"It's hand spun wool," Cherry bragged.

"May I try it on?" Mariah asked in a mischievous voice.

"Yeah, sure, give it a go, girl," Cherry offered.

Mariah lifted the beautiful garment and draped it over her shoulders. It was long and fit like a poncho or a cape. "I feel powerful," she said in a near whisper.

"That is the magic of this cloak," Cherry admitted. "And you'll need a bit of magic, you know, on a quest."

"So you're willing to trade?" Mariah asked.

"I am if you are," Cherry nodded.

Mariah raised an eyebrow. "My apple is very special," she said again.

"Mmm hmmm," Cherry murmured, an uncertain concession.

"I'll be needing that charm round your neck too," Mariah said suddenly and assertively. "Your little silver acorn."

Cherry nodded. "Indeed you will be needing it," she declared. "It will bring you harmony and balance. If I'll be willing to part with it."

Mariah raised her eyebrows, questioning, waiting. But Cherry said nothing. So Mariah pulled out her cell phone. "This apple is pure crystal!" she exclaimed. "And worth a lot of money! I'll bet I can find one online to show you what it's worth."

Cherry raised her hand. "But will you find one such as myself who will give you the magic of her possessions in exchange for this apple?"

Mariah was struck dumb by this proclamation. One such as myself--the words rang in her ears. Was Cherry indeed an angel? A cherub in disguise? She considered her warning then raised her own hand. "I am the daughter of Charlie and Samantha Easter," she said in a low voice. "I come from a legacy of mysticism and magic. I am offering you a good trade; take it or leave it."

Cherry's head reared back. She seemed stunned, but she recovered quickly to laugh. "Well done, dear, I must admit." She shook her head in surrender. "Thus it shall be--my cloak and my acorn for your crystal apple." She took her necklace off, and handed it to Mariah.

Mariah extended her hand and they shook on the deal. Then Mariah gleefully wrapped her arms around herself pulling the cloak closer. Cherry caught up the apple as if lifting a crystal ball to gaze into. "I see you finding many surprises in your travels, young Mary," Cherry announced.

"My name's not Mary."

"No, but I'm close, aren't I?" Cherry said with a sly wink.

"Yes," Mariah conceded. "You're very close." And yet, she felt she wanted to keep her name a secret right now, even from this benefactor, as if her name were another piece of currency that she wasn't going to release at this moment.

She went out into the night in her boots and her cloak, an acorn in her pocket and her pack slung comfortable over her shoulder. She glanced up the street and could see the bridge lit with dozens of yellow lights. She turned left toward it, leaving Motel 6 in her wake.

***

In the first light of dawn, Mariah sat huddled in her newly acquired cloak on a bench in front of the Rune Stone Museum. To pass the time, she prayed the rosary, counting the decades on her fingers. When she finished the traditional five decades, she pulled out her cell phone, went online and began to search for the thimble. There were hundreds of thimbles out in cyberspace, it was a wonder they'd found it twice already. When she saw the sun peeking over the buildings, she stopped searching and sent her mother a text. "gone for walk. b rt back."

Chapter Eleven

Samantha awoke and was surprised to find her daughter was no longer beside her in the motel bed. Dale was still snoring, so she rose softly and moved slowly, despite the anxiety flooding her chest and limbs at Mariah's absence. She tiptoed into the bathroom and found no evidence that Mariah had showered. Certainly the teenager would not have gone off without washing and styling her hair. She crept back out to the main room and as quietly as possible she cracked open the door. It was a cold but sunny day and there was no trace of Mariah on the passageway or parking lot. She closed the door clumsily and Dale stirred. "What time is it?" he asked.

"Seven thirty," she said. "And Mariah's missing."

***

The sign outside the museum said it didn't open until ten. Mariah wondered if she really could wait that long. Her mother must be worried by now, though she hadn't tried to call her yet. She was getting hungry. The pie and ice cream had certainly tided her over, but it was no substitute for a hearty breakfast. She yawned and stretched and looked about when she saw a man in a blue jacket get out of a white car and head to the museum entrance. He fingered a jumble of keys in his hand, seemingly searching for just the right one. He finally isolated a large copper colored key and held it out in front of himself as if it were a divining rod leading the way. Mariah jumped up.

"Sir," she called to him. "Do you work at the museum? Are you going inside?"

He seemed a little startled at her greeting. "Can I help you?" he said stiffly and formally, as one would speak to a homeless person or intruder.

"Oh, yes, please," Mariah pleaded. "I wanted to go in to see the Rune stone, but I don't know if I can wait till ten. My mother will be very worried about me---you know I left the motel in the middle of the night and--"

"How old are you?" he asked. "Have you been sleeping on the streets?"

"No, of course not," Mariah said defensively. "I just wanted to see the Rune Stone before we go back to California. I'm here with my mother and brother, and I need to get back to them soon. I won't stay long; I want to see it and then I'll go. Ten minutes tops."

The man rolled his eyes, but as soon as he unlocked the door he stepped aside and motioned her in. "Thank you," she said. "I really appreciate it."

The man led the way into a large room, flipping on light switches as they walked. "Here it is," he said.

The stone was encased in a large glass display vault. Mariah approached it quickly and stood inches from its surface. She took a deep breath and closed her eyes, meditating the way her mother had taught her to do. She wanted to feel something. She hoped that the emanations from the stone would somehow guide her, provide a clue as to what she should do next. She held her breath but--nothing. She felt nothing.

She opened her eyes to find the man staring intently at her. "Are you all right?" he asked pointedly. It was obvious he was suspicious. There would be no alone time with this stone,

Mariah realized.

"Do you think this stone has some spiritual significance?" she asked.

He exhaled audibly, looking annoyed. "No."

Mariah bit her lip to hide her disappointment. "But it says 'Ave Maria.' I can see that right there," she said pointing.

"Yes, and that has great historical significance," the man told her, suddenly jumping to life at this chance to discuss the stone. "That reference to the prayer has been instrumental in the dating of the stone since there was only a small window of time when Latin and Runic characters would have appeared together like this. And that window corresponds perfectly with the date carved into the stone. It's one of the essential keys in proving the authenticity."

"I see," Mariah said, nodding.

"Yes," he continued, "it was before the Reformation, and in fact carved during the Middle Ages when the Mary cults were at their height."

"The Mary cults?" Mariah repeated.

"Reverence and devotion to Mary swelled during the Middle Ages, akin to goddess worship."

"Oh!--and this stone was evidence of their devotion to Mary?"

"Doubtful, but impossible to know," the man said. "This stone was most likely placed as a marker of how far the expedition was able to come. The farthest point in their journey before disease stopped them."

"So I guess," Mariah mused, "it's a monument to their perseverance and sacrifice."

The man raised his hands as if commanding her to stop. "It's a marker, that's all we can say for sure. What the company was thinking or feeling at the time is pure speculation."

"I like to speculate," Mariah said in a disappointed voice. "It's fun."

"Don't get me wrong," the man said. "Speculation is actually a big part of scientific research. Scientists are much more creative than people give them credit for. First comes a hypothesis, but then scientists have to do the hard work of finding out if the hypothesis—the speculation--is true or not. Things that can't be proved or disproved through the scientific method aren't things that scientists are going to explore. How the people felt at that time--I can't prove or disprove that. It makes a nice story, but I can't tell you whether it's true or not. The only thing I can pass on to you with certainty is that there is some evidence that this stone served as a marker for how far the expedition was able to progress. If the stone is genuine, then their journey ended here."

Mariah nodded sadly. "And I guess this is where my journey is ending too."

The man spread his arms in a show of ignorance. "Hey, I don't know what you're going through, miss, but whatever it is--you're young--give it some time. My hypothesis is that you've got a lot of journeying ahead of you."

Mariah blinked her eyes rapidly to disperse her tears. "Thank you for your time," she said softly.

As she walked back out to the street, Mariah could feel her cell phone vibrating in her pocket. She pulled it out and saw Dale's face on the screen. "Hey," she said answering it.

"Where the heck are you?" Dale blurted. "Your mother is worried sick."

"I sent her a text," Mariah pleaded.

"Two hours ago," he retorted. "Look," he continued, his voice softening. "I know this is a hard time right now for you, but think of your mom--"

"I know; I'm sorry." she whined.

"So I'm still waiting for you to answer my question: where are you? Are you lost?"

"I'm not lost; I know my way back," she said feeling annoyed. "I just have to cross over the bridge and it's a ten minute walk. I--"

"Over the bridge?" he said incredulous. "You mean the bridge that's out? You crossed over an unsound bridge?"

Mariah pushed her hair out of her eyes. "The bridge is fine, Dale! That mean little man was lying to us!"

Dale snorted. "Big surprise there," he said sarcastically. "The guy is running credit card scams, so of course he's going to lie to us about a bridge. What a jackass! But that doesn't explain what you're doing on the other side of the bridge. What are you doing crossing bridges when your mom thinks you're sleeping beside her, huh?"

"I'm 17 years old, Dale," Mariah said tartly. "I've been walking since I was 8 months. I can cross a bridge."

"Jeez, Mariah, you have no clue how dangerous it can be to walk around a strange place by yourself like that. You sit tight and I'll come pick you up."

"Dale, I'm half way to the bridge now. I'll be back at the motel before you get your shoes on."

"Don't you smart mouth me," he said. "I have got my shoes on! Your mom is in the shower. She wanted to run out searching for you in her night gown, but I talked her down."

"Why didn't she call? She'd see I was all right," Mariah asked, picking up her pace.

"What do you think, Mariah?" Dale continued. "Of course she called. At least a half dozen times. Check out the missed calls and you'll see. Or didn't you realize that your phone was off?"

Mariah sighed. "It was on vibrate," she said in a softer, humbler tone. "I'm sorry; I've got to cross a street and then I'll be over the bridge and back. Like I said--ten minutes. Probably less."

"Okay, you sure you don't want me to come get you?"

"Dale, it's fine, okay? Please don't be mad at me!"

"I'm sorry, Mariah," he said in a more conciliatory voice. "It's just that your mom seems so tired. You know what I'm thinking--this van has had a good run --I'm thinking I'll sell it to a used lot here, and get something new when we get home. Then we can buy some plane tickets and jet out of here today. We could be in California tonight. It would be for the best."

"Really?" Mariah said. "But you love that van--"

"Where'd you get that idea? This was Jeannette's pick. I could do with something a little more streamlined."

"Oh. Okay. Whatever you want."

"Listen," Dale said. "Your mom's going to be out of the bathroom soon, so pick up your pace!"

"Bye, Dale," she said glumly and she hung up.

She was at the base of the bridge, loitering there for a moment or two, feeling bad that her dream of finding the thimble was going to end here. Home by tonight--that sounded good, but it made her sad to go home to a house without her father. But what did she want? What could fill this empty place in her heart?

She strolled a few feet to sink onto a bench near the riverbank. The phone still in her hand, she logged on to goggle and entered the phrase "collectable thimbles." A slew of possibilities popped on to her screen. But she'd been down this road before. With a few quick words she described the Easter family thimble: 18 karat gold, double eagle-etched design. She held her breath, and then a possibility emerged. She clicked on a link and there it was. She leaned forward to study the screen more closely--was this the ad posted by the little man a week ago?--No! It was a new link, a new ad, and a new photo!--but there was no mistaking the lower case e at the smaller hawk's eyelid. This was her thimble, and it was being advertised by a seller in Connecticut.

She felt her heart in her throat, afraid of what she was thinking. It was there, she was sure that was it! But she couldn't ask her mother and brother to journey any further. She had to let go sometime, didn't she? Or did she have to break away? There was no reason why she couldn't carry on by herself. She had everything she needed: boots, a cloak, a pack and of course the credit card her father had indulgently given her for her 16th birthday.

She took a deep breath, leaning back on the bench and staring up at the sky. Her mother and brother would never allow this. For the first time she realized it wasn't their choice, not by a long shot. She was nearly eighteen years old; it was time for her to show some independence. Was she ready? Could she really imagine starting out on her own?

She caught sight of a large bird gliding slowly, circling, circling above the water. It was a hawk. It was descending slowly, and she stood to get a better look. She followed as the bird slid across the sky, flying away from the bridge and coming her way. She was fully engrossed as if she had a form of tunnel vision, her gaze focused only on the hawk, her thoughts blissfully non existent, her attention fully captured by this winged creature. Unknowing, she was the hawk, safe in the cool morning air, supported fully by the draft that flowed over and under her wings. She was peaceful and content, she was hawk, she was--suddenly snatched by the collar and pulled back from advancing traffic. "Hey," a loud voice said, "you nearly got yourself hit by a bus! Watch yourself."

Suddenly she was Mariah again and she was at the edge of the pavement on the landing to the bridge. Trucks, buses, and SUV's rumbled in front of her at break neck speed. Not bothering to turn around, she blurted to her unseen savior, "You saved my life!"

She heard her benefactor snort. "Fine, now don't go wasting it!"

She turned but there was no one there in the clump of people rushing down the sidewalk who appeared to be the one speaking to her. She felt shaken and confused, but the direction was clear. *Don't waste your life, don't waste your time. Become your own person now.* "Excuse me," she shouted to a woman striding by, "is there a bus station near here?"

***

Samantha came out of the registration office at the Motel 6 to find Dale leaning against the door of his van, texting on his cell phone. "Are you talking to Mariah?" she asked.

"No," he confessed, coloring slightly as he admitted it. "No, I was texting with Luisa."

"Oh," Samantha said obviously surprised.

"Yeah, she texted me first this time," he sounded eager and happy, but a little embarrassed.

Samantha smiled. "That's sweet; I'm glad--but it's been over forty minutes, hasn't it? Since you talked to Mariah? She said it would only be ten minutes, didn't she?"

Dale could see his stepmother was blinking back tears. "She probably underestimated the time it would take. Go ahead and call her, Sam," he said. "It's okay, I'm sure she's got her phone turned up now."

Samantha nodded rapidly as she pulled her own phone from her purse. "Okay, you know me; I've never depended much on a phone like this." Dale watched as she punched in the speed dial, then lifted the device to her face to hear it ring. They waited in silence, staring at each other's faces. "She's not answering," she said, the tears streaming down her cheeks.

"Okay, look, Sam," Dale said quickly. "I'll get in the van and drive over near the bridge, but you've got to wait here in case she's taking a different route or something, okay? Now keep your phone out and call me when she gets back or if you hear from her. My phone will be right on the dash. The second I see her, I'm calling you, okay? It'll be fine. In fact, do this--go into Denny's, have a seat, place your order, and send Mariah a text telling her where you are. It'll be fine; you'll see."

Dale drove away and Samantha stood firm in the parking lot of the motel for several minutes. She stared at her phone, then she tried to call on her phone, then she put her phone back into her purse. Finally she decided that Dale was right. She walked slowly across the parking lot and into the Denny's. She ordered coffee, and then began the laborious task of typing a text with her thumbs.

***

At the bus station, Mariah felt her phone vibrating in her pocket, but she didn't answer it. She knew what she was doing was going to upset her mother something awful. *I should feel guilty.*

She had never traveled alone before. *I should feel scared.*

Thoughts of how she *should* feel swirled in her head, but the fact was she had no idea what her true feelings were. She was cool. Her hands were steady as she pulled out her credit card. She could not fathom why she felt such certainty, but she knew what she needed to do.

The line in front of her dwindled. She approached the ticket window. Her voice was calm. "One way to Hartford please," she said.

"Leaving in seven minutes," the cashier responded. "Better hurry."

***

On the bus, Mariah ate a processed ham and cheese sandwich she'd bought from a vending machine at the station. It was awful, but it took the edge off her hunger, giving her the fortitude to do what she needed to do next. She pulled her cell phone from her hip pocket.

The bus was uncrowded; she'd been able to secure a seat to herself where she could spread out her few belongings. She stared out the bus window, looking but not seeing pastures and farmhouses as they drifted by. She wanted to say a prayer, but her mind was blank, her heart thumping. She took a deep breath and pushed in her mother's number.

"Mariah!" Her mother's voice nearly shrieked her name. "Where are you? Are you with Dale?"

"Dale? No--"

"He went out looking for you in the van," Samantha continued. "Call him so he can come pick you up."

"That won't work, Mom," Mariah said slowly. "See, I'm on a bus to Connecticut."

"Excuse me?" Samantha yelled.

Mariah kept her voice deliberately low. "Please don't be upset--"

"I don't understand. You told Dale you were headed back to the motel, that you'd be here in ten minutes. That was nearly an hour ago! This doesn't make any sense! Mariah! I have never known you to tell a lie! Not even when you were a little girl! I don't understand."

"I didn't lie, Mom," Mariah whined defensively. "I changed my mind is all. I'm sorry; I don't mean to upset you--but I'm on a quest--"

"Fuck this quest business," Samantha said harshly and Mariah felt thrown back in her seat. "You're not your father," her mother went on, "you're not like him, you're not going to run across the country like this every time things get a little rough at home--"

Mariah could feel a franticness in her mother's voice, and an infectious wave of anxiety passed through her too. "What are you talking about?"

"This isn't something to talk about on the phone. Dale has a plan so we can fly home tonight. Just come back to us, baby."

Mariah felt stung. "I'm not a baby anymore," she retorted.

"Mariah, please, please don't do this."

Hearing the pleading timber of her mother's voice sent her from anger to guilt. But she would not be swayed. "Mom, the bus is on its way," she said. "I *can't* come back now."

"Of course you can, dear," Samantha informed her, her voice suddenly steady. "Your father used to do this all the time. You get up and tell the driver you want to get off. He'll do that for you. He'll pull over and let you off. Then you call Dale and he'll come get you. We can handle this."

"My father used to do this--? What are you talking about?" she asked.

"Never mind. Just get off the bus."

Mariah leaned back. She recognized this voice. It spoke in short, imperative sentences. On those occasions when she'd gone to visit her mother at work, she'd been both impressed and amused to discover that her mother had this secret persona, that Samantha could affect a commanding presence at will. When the room was noisy, when kids were rowdy, her mother would pull it out: the voice. It wasn't a matter of volume; it was a force of tone. *Return to your desks. We need quiet voices now.*

But Mariah had never heard her mother use this voice when addressing her. Samantha never needed to—because Mariah had always been a good girl, cooperative and reasonable.

Hearing this voice stunned Mariah. Was her mother justified? Mariah knew she was not being cooperative. But was she being unreasonable? Mariah wasn't sure, but at this moment she knew it didn't matter. Crazy or not, she felt compelled to continue her search.

"Mom," she said firmly. "I'm not going to get off the bus now, *because I don't want to.* I'm going to Connecticut."

"Connecticut," Samantha cried, her forceful voice lost. "Why there, of all places, why Connecticut?"

"Because, Mom--that's where the thimble is!"

Chapter Twelve

Luisa floated in the heated pool in their back yard in New Haven. She loved the feel of the water enfolding her skin. She'd always loved swimming because the pressure of the water made her feel secure.

She thought of Dale in Minnesota now, eating pancakes with purple syrup and red and blue and purple berries. He seemed to find it amusing to take photos of his meals with his phone and send them to her with a text. She wondered if this were some form of courtship ritual that she, with her limited experience, was unaware of. This morning he'd sent her the photo of the colorful pancakes from a Denny's in Minnesota. Last week he'd sent a photo of a plate of Mexican food from what he said was his favorite restaurant in Sedona. He said the enchiladas had mole sauce on them. She'd never heard of mole sauce. Her mother said it was very good, and that she'd look for a recipe so she could try it. Her mother loved cooking, so that promised to be fun.

On Sunday, Dale sent photos from a farmers' market somewhere in the Midwest. He took pictures of strawberries, chili peppers, onions and corn. It was all very pretty.

Luisa had never corresponded with a man in this manner before. Most of her correspondence was of a professional nature, or at least intellectual. She often received emails from students and teachers asking about her perceptions of the world, and how her sensory challenges allowed her to perceive input in a way that is different from the way the neuro-typical person might perceive it. Luisa appreciated the directness of these questions; she knew the people asking wanted to be able to understand the people in their own lives who have autism. Luisa patiently answered these questions. She knew it was an important part of her mission. For herself, she liked to correspond with people like Samantha and Craig with whom she could discuss her doctoral dissertation and continuing study of the similarities between the mystical writings of monotheists and Buddhists.

But Dale was different. He wanted to know what novels she read, what movies she enjoyed, and what music she listened to. He texted her lines that Stephen Colbert had said the night before on his TV show, and yeah, he was pretty funny. She started watching him too some nights and then she'd text Dale before he could watch it in his later time zone. "Just a teaser," she'd say. "I won't give the rest away."

This morning Dale said they were headed to Connecticut, looking for his half sister who had taken off without him and Samantha. Luisa loved Samantha, and hoped she wasn't too upset about this. Somehow she felt it would all turn out all right for Samantha and her family, but she imagined this was very hard for Samantha right now, so close after her husband's death.

Nonetheless, Luisa couldn't stop thinking about the other thing Dale had said. He said that since they were coming to the east coast, wouldn't it be great if they took a side trip to New Haven so he could meet her. Luisa sunk into the pool submerging her face and head. She felt herself trembling and she jerked herself half out of the water. Yelling wordlessly and clutching her arms across her chest, her hands gripped her shoulders. She could hear her own throat screaming and screaming like a goat. She thrust her hand into her mouth and bit her thumb hard. This stopped the screaming and though her thumb bled it didn't hurt. Her breathing slowed and she sunk back down into the shallow end of the water. She rocked.

***

As they drove east, Samantha felt compelled to check her cell phone for messages every fifteen minutes or so, but there was no word from Mariah. She prayed the rosary constantly, counting the decades on a single decade rosary crafted from Connemara marble that her mother had bought in a gift shop in Killarney decades ago.

As they were driving through Wisconsin, Samantha noticed a message from Luisa's mother Anna, asking Samantha to call her as soon as possible. She had a lively Facebook relationship with Anna but had not actually seen or spoken to her in several years. Yet she and Anna considered themselves close, and Anna had sent a large spray of flowers to Charlie's funeral. Something told Samantha not to mention this message to Dale.

When they stopped for gas as they were entering Illinois, Samantha made a discreet call to Anna from the women's restroom where Dale wouldn't hear. "Anna? It's Samantha, dear. So good to hear your voice!"

"Oh, Samantha! I'm so happy to hear from you too. You know you have been in my thoughts so much since Charlie died, and now Luisa tells me that Mariah is missing?"

"Oh," Samantha said, almost embarrassed to admit more troubles. "Well, she's not exactly missing. She's heading for Connecticut, and we want to head her off. We're all so vulnerable right now. I'm sure she's not thinking straight."

"Nonetheless, it's very upsetting, Samantha. I'm so sorry it's all happening like this," Anna said with emphasis.

"Thank you, Anna, it was very sweet of you to call. I didn't even know any one knew, but I guess Dale told Luisa."

"Yes," Anna said with a strange sharpness. "Dale and Luisa." She paused and Samantha felt chilled. "You know I love you, Samantha," Anna resumed, "and I've always trusted you, especially in matters relating to my daughter. I don't want to be harsh, what with all you're going through right now--"

Anna paused again and Samantha braced herself, knowing what was coming next. Yet she stayed silent, waiting for Anna's emotion to hit her.

"Samantha," Anna said forcefully, "what game are you playing at?--playing match maker to my daughter and your step son! Are you out of your mind?"

Samantha took a deep breath, remembering how powerful and intimidating Anna could be when she first met her, back when Luisa was her 11-year-old student and she was a newly divorced, suddenly pregnant teacher who had no tenure in the district. She had more confidence now. "Anna," she said steadily, "you sound angry."

"I *am* angry!" Anna exclaimed. "What are you thinking? You know Luisa could never handle a relationship like this--especially with a neuro-typical man!"

"Now you sound a little scared," Samantha said, speaking slowly to keep herself calm.

"Oh, Samantha, I don't want Luisa to get hurt! I'm not angry with you--or with Dale. Not really. I know you both just lost Charlie, and certainly Dale is looking for someone to fill that emptiness he must feel. But Samantha!"

Samantha took another deep breath, afraid she might inadvertently blurt out that Dale was also recovering from a divorce. No, that information was completely unnecessary. "Anna, let me tell you what happened: Dale saw a photo of Luisa in my office and he was smitten. I'll admit you may be right; he'd just lost his father, and the idea of a fairy tale romance with a beautiful girl in a photograph may have been too much. I cautioned him that Luisa has autism, but I still gave him her address because I thought she could help him through his loss. I know it's a big burden to place on Luisa--"

"It's not only a burden, it's scaring her. She's never had a boyfriend before and, sure, she's enjoying his attention, but it's different for her. It's not what she's used to. I think she's overwhelmed," Anna argued.

"Well it is overwhelming the first time you have a man's attention, don't you remember? Oh, heck, it can be overwhelming any time you've got a man's attention. But Anna!" Samantha exclaimed. "Don't you remember? It can be so much fun! Now if Luisa isn't having fun with Dale, then she needs to tell him to back off. It's only been a few weeks, a few very intense weeks for Dale, I have to say. But he's a grown-up, if she tells him to slow down--or even to stop--he'll manage. Of course he'll be disappointed, but that's okay, that's the risk we all take when we put ourselves out there."

"Well," Anna said in a magnanimous tone, "she doesn't want to hurt him."

Samantha rolled her eyes, but forged on. "Is that what she's telling you?"

Anna sighed audibly. "Well, no, but--I don't know."

Samantha wondered if it were Luisa or her mother who was really scared and overwhelmed. "Anna," she said gently, "I'll remind Dale that Luisa is a special woman, highly intelligent and spiritually gifted, but if Luisa wants him to back off, she has to be the one who tells him so. It's not something I can do and it's not something you can do for her. You know I'm right--you know Luisa wouldn't want it any other way."

"Yes, of course," Anna admitted. "Luisa would be mortified to hear me interfering like this. But you're a mother: you understand why I worry."

Samantha blinked back tears. "Of course I understand." They were both silent for a moment, sharing this moment, and

Samantha wished she could take Anna's hand, to comfort herself as much as the other woman.

"Oh Samantha," Anna gushed, "I wish I could give you a big hug right now. You must be so worried about Mariah!"

"Anna, I knew you would understand better than anyone."

"Sweetie," Anna continued, "I know you're right that it's up to Luisa how she handles her relationship with Dale, but don't you think it's kind of early for you both to come back here so he can meet her?"

"We're not coming to New Haven, Anna. We're headed for Hartford and then Mystic to find Mariah."

"Yes, Sam," Anna said, "but Dale told Luisa that since you're heading for the east coast you may as well come down to New Haven to see her, and then even visit with some of the Easter family."

"He hasn't mentioned that to me, Anna," Samantha said, unable to suppress a deep sigh. "I want to find my daughter and fly home to Sacramento! I hope you don't mind if I miss New Haven this trip."

"I understand entirely--and you know you'd be welcome anytime, but this thing between Luisa and Dale is moving so fast!"

"Everything is moving too fast for me right now!" Samantha lamented. "But dear, please remember, Luisa believes that everything she experiences has meaning and purpose for her. She feels everything in her life was designed before her birth."

"I don't know if I buy that, Samantha!" Anna interjected.

"It doesn't matter if you believe it, Anna," Samantha replied. "It only matters that Luisa believes it. She and Dale may have played this out on the astral planes before any of us even incarnated on this planet. And whether their relationship develops into romance or friendship or heartbreak--it's what Luisa wants for herself. She came to experience life! We all did! And this is a very big and important part of the human experience. We can't deprive her of this."

"And no matter how scared you are, Samantha, Mariah is acting out the same mystery play boys and girls have enacted for millennia--the coming of age drama-- finding her own way in the universe. It's hard, but I think we'll all survive it."

"I know, Anna. And thank you."

***

"Dale," Samantha asked slowly as she got back into the van, "are you planning to go on to New Haven once we find Mariah?"

Dale blushed. "I--uh--why--I mean how--?"

Samantha didn't know whether to laugh out loud or cry at the poignancy of his desire. "Luisa's mother called me. I was talking with her in the bathroom."

He lowered his eyebrows. "Is there a problem?"

"No, not really--well, she's anxious. You know Luisa lives with her mother, and she always has ever since she was adopted nearly 27 years ago." Samantha paused. "I'm not sure I've made it clear that Luisa has very special needs. She really can't live completely independently. She makes good money now teaching at an Ivy League university, but she'll always need someone to help her cook and clean--and even to bathe and dress herself."

Dale leaned forward with interest. "Is she paralyzed in some way? I didn't realize-"

"No, no, it's not like that," Samantha said quickly. "It's more like she can't control her own movements all the time. So she needs some help. But she can walk and she swims--she loves to swim--and she does a little cooking when her mother or an assistant is there to supervise. And of course she types independently, and she teaches all her classes online."

"I think I understand." he said. He turned the key in the ignition, and checked the mirrors so he could pull the van out of its parking space. "I guess her mother is worried that I'll meet her and be disappointed or even shocked and--"

"And maybe you will be, Dale," Samantha interjected, touching his shoulder. "Even if she were an ordinary woman, corresponding online is a lot different than having a face to face relationship. You might be disappointed for all kinds of reasons. Or she might be disappointed in you."

"I know that," Dale said as he maneuvered the van toward the exit.

"Oh, you say that, Dale, but no, you don't know, you can't know right now. You have to get there and let it happen. Right now, I suspect you're falling in love with Luisa online. And I'd be just as worried about you if Luisa wasn't autistic. But I'm also happy and excited for you too. Still I want you to consider if going to meet her now is a little too soon, no matter how close we get to New Haven."

Dale was silent for a moment as he waited for a chance to pull the van into heavy traffic. "I don't know, Sam. I think it's up to me and Luisa," he said finally.

"Well, yes, exactly; that's what I just spent the last fifteen minutes telling her mother," Samantha prattled rapidly, trying to keep up with her own thoughts. "Anna accepted what I had to say. It'll be fine. It will be. So really, if you want to go meet her now--" Her voice trailed off for a moment, then she took a deep breath and resumed. "Oh heck, I'd love for you to go meet her tonight if we could. I may as well admit it," she said.

He turned to her abruptly. "Are you crying, Sam?"

"Oh, Dale," she said, "I keep thinking: I fell in love with your father on first sight. I didn't even believe that kind of thing was possible until I met him. I think if you fell in love with Luisa's photograph, well, you've got as good a chance as anybody else of forging a good solid relationship. I can't wait to see how this story is going to develop."

He grinned, then seeing a break in traffic pulled onto the road. "So you're in? We'll head to New Haven once we find Mariah?" he asked.

"Oh, I don't know, Dale," she whined. "I'd like to say yes, but I'm so tired. I really do want to go home."

He accelerated on the two-lane road. "That's okay, Sam, I understand," he agreed. "I can buy plane tickets for you and Mariah when we get to Connecticut--"

"You don't have to buy me anything, sweetie; I can buy my own plane tickets."

He reached out to pat her knee while keeping his eyes on the road. "Listen, Sam, I know you and my dad sometimes had trouble making ends meet and I don't ever want you to hesitate to ask me for money. You know I've got a good job and--"

"Dale," Samantha interrupted him. "I'm touched that you worry about Mariah and me, but there's something I need you to know." She paused to take a deep breath. "I, uh, I had an insurance policy on your father's life. Yeah, so now I guess I'll be able to cash it in. I don't think we're ever going to have to worry about money again. It'll pay for my retirement and for Mariah's education and then some."

"Samantha!" Dale exclaimed, stealing a quick glance at her. "That's great! I'm so happy for you!"

Samantha started crying again. "I bought it years ago, Dale, because your father was such a dare devil, and I didn't want to be left a single mom. You know I had a baby and all, and I've been paying the premiums all these years--"

"That's good, Sam! Why are you crying?"

"I never wanted him to die like this," she sobbed. "Now I'm rich because of it! I feel so guilty."

"Oh, Sam," he assured her, "You did the right thing buying a policy to take care of yourself and Mariah. That was smart; don't feel bad about it."

She rubbed at the tears with her fist. "I know, I felt so bad, I haven't even told anybody." She stopped for a moment to consider. "Well, I told Craig. He's the only one I've told."

Dale slowed as they neared an intersection. "Have you spoken to Craig since the funeral?" he asked. "I'll bet you'd feel better if you gave him a call."

She nodded. "I think you're right. I'll do that at the next stop."

Chapter Thirteen

Mariah turned off her phone and slept all night on the bus. She dreamt of a hawk speaking to her in an Irish brogue, but she couldn't remember what the bird said.

When the bus arrived in Hartford, Mariah went to the counter for help plotting the next leg of her trip. "I need to get to a town called Mystic," she told the cashier. The young woman at the counter pushed her glasses further up on her nose. She looked barely older than Mariah herself. She had bright red unruly hair tied back with a rubber band. "There's a local leaving tomorrow at ten that passes through Mystic. Do you want a ticket on that?"

"Not till tomorrow?" Mariah said, feeling a stab of anxiety at having to find food and lodging for the night. "Nothing sooner?"

"Not here, miss," the woman informed her. "But I'm thinking Greyline might have some tourist trips that go through there. They've got an office right up the street. Ask them for their trips to Gungywamp."

"Gungywamp?" Mariah repeated the strange word, suddenly afraid that this young woman was playing a trick on her. "That doesn't even sound like a real word."

"It's Gaelic, miss," the woman said, a tinge of indignation in her voice.

"I'm sorry, I didn't mean to doubt you," Mariah apologized. "My grandfather was Irish but no one I know speaks Gaelic."

"That's all right," the red haired girl assured it. "It means 'church of the people' and it's like Stonehenge or Newgrange."

"Stonehenge?" Mariah exclaimed. "But how can that be? Were there ancient Celts here in New England?"

"The stone structures are like ones built in the Middle Ages in Ireland by the Culdee monks. They were driven from their homes in the 9th century by Norse invaders," the girl babbled quickly. "So they came here and they built their own ceremonial stone huts--shaped like beehives! And they're built to track the sun so the light falls inside at the fall and spring equinoxes."

"That's amazing," Mariah said.

"You've got to go check it out, miss," the red head said hastily. "I've got a line forming behind you."

"Oh," Mariah said turning to look. "Okay, thank you."

***

Dale and Samantha picked Craig up at the Cleveland airport. "I'm so happy you came out to meet us," Samantha gushed as he embraced her at the gate.

He pulled his ticket out of his pack. "This is a round trip ticket right?" he said in a warning voice. "Because there's no way the Craig vehicle is going to drive all the way back to California in that van of yours, Dale."

Dale laughed. "The plan right now is to ditch this van somewhere back here so we can all fly home." He paused. "Though our plans are pretty fluid right now." Samantha smiled when she saw he was blushing. "Let's go get your luggage," he added.

"No, I have no luggage," Craig announced unceremoniously. "This is it," he said, lifting a small backpack. "When I heard Samantha's voice on the phone, it resonated with me--I knew I had to come out here. I don't know why. But I know this stay will be brief --for me anyway. I can't say what you all are planning to do next."

They began walking through the terminal to the parking lot.

"Craig, is Mariah all right? Can you see where she is?" Samantha asked.

"I don't know," Craig said in a flat voice. "Though I think if she weren't all right I would be able to sense that. You have to understand, Samantha, I came out here to support you. Mariah's more or less on her own now."

"We'll be able to find her, won't we? She's not answering her phone!"

"Of course we're going to find her, Sam," Dale said calmly. "Mariah's a smart girl."

Craig held his hand in appreciation toward Dale. "Do you see Samantha? Dale is not worried; he has confidence in Mariah's own wisdom. You are allowing your judgment to be clouded with fear. When you allow yourself to be quiet and to get back in touch with your own heart, you'll be able to feel that Mariah has never left you."

They arrived at the van, and Dale took Craig's pack and stashed it in back with the suitcases. "Is this Mariah's bag?" Craig asked, indicating a hot pink suitcase with her name monogrammed on it. "She's not going to get very far if she didn't take her belongings with her."

Samantha tapped his arm. "She has Charlie's credit card," she revealed with a roll of her eyes. "She could travel for years if I pay the bills, or I could pull it and end the journey now."

Craig smiled. "But you're not going to do that, are you?"

"I'm thinking about it," Samantha said. "It would serve her right for worrying me like this."

"Samantha, you know this is her time," Craig said. "It's only a dry run, but the time is coming for her to break free and do the work she needs to do. She's preparing herself."

"Why can't she prepare herself back in our nice safe back yard?" Samantha wailed.

Craig laughed. "She could prepare herself anywhere in any way she sees fit. But she has to do it. And if she doesn't do it now, you don't know what she'll do next time." He raised his eyebrows at her as she started to interrupt him. "Ah--" he said, laughing again, anticipating her objections. "Give her this space."

Samantha sighed. "You want to sit in the front? There's more leg room."

"It's fine back here. You sit up next to Dale."

Dale had been watching their heated discussion though he couldn't hear everything that had been said. "Okay, Sam?" he asked.

"I'm good," she acknowledged with a nod to Craig.

"So where are we going?" Craig asked.

"To Mystic, Connecticut," Dale told him as he pulled out of the parking lot. "It's where the thimble was last seen--you know, online."

Craig settled himself into the back seat, stretching out his long arms and legs. "So now, Samantha, Dale: tell me about this woman who stole Mariah's thimble."

"Oh," Samantha mused, running her hands through her

hair, "it all happened so fast, I'm not sure I got a good look at her. She was tall, skinny and very strong. That's all I know for sure."

"She was freaky looking," Dale said. "Albino-like skin and hair, but Kelly green eyes."

"And nobody knew who she was?" Craig asked.

Samantha passed Craig a bag of pretzels. "We didn't know who she was or how she knew we were having a funeral reception," Samantha said.

"She was at the cemetery," Dale interjected. "She must have followed us to your house from there."

Samantha accepted a handful of pretzels from Craig. "She was at the cemetery? I didn't see her there."

"Yeah," Dale affirmed as he stopped the van at a red light. "She came walking across the lawn, then she stood at the back and she just sobbed." He turned to face Craig, gesturing dramatically. "Tears streamed down her cheeks, her whole body trembled. But not a sound. It was eerie."

Samantha sat up a little straighter. "She sounds like a banshee."

"A banshee?" Dale repeated. "A screaming banshee?"

The light turned green, and Dale started the van up again. Samantha shook her head. "Obviously there's no such thing."

Craig paused in his pretzel-munching. "What exactly is a banshee?"

"Just another movie monster," Dale said dismissively.

"Oh, no," Samantha said. "A banshee is a type of Irish fairy."

"An Irish fairy?" Craig said, apparently surprised.

"Yes, it's a particular type of fairy, often associated with particular families," Samantha explained. "It shows up at the death of a family member. You know—to keen."

Craig laughed. "Keen?"

"To wail and cry and grieve in a conspicuous manner. The louder the keening, the more beloved the deceased."

"This woman was a silent keener," Dale informed her. "That's not saying much for Dad."

"Well, I didn't say she actually was a banshee," Samantha said defensively. "I mean, after all, it's a myth. There's no such thing."

"And yet," Craig said with a mischievous gleam, "you manifested one."

"*I* manifested one?" Samantha exclaimed. "Why me?"

"Hey, you're the only Irishwoman in this car," Craig insisted. "Am I right, Dale?"

"That's correct, Craig," Dale confirmed as he glanced at Samantha's friend in the rear view mirror. "So, if anybody's family has attracted a banshee it would have to be yours, Ms O'Malley."

Samantha was silent for a moment, realizing no one had called her by her maiden name in nearly two decades. No one except Charlie.

Craig seemed to sense her mood as he leaned forward to squeeze her shoulder. "So," he said boisterously to Dale, "do you think there's a pizza parlor between here and Connecticut? I'm getting a hankering for pepperoni."

Dale laughed. "I'll see what I can do."

***

Mariah joined a tour of people who were on their way to Gungywamp. The guide stood at the front of the bus talking about the Indian tribes in the area, how the area had been a rich hunting ground for them as well as a sheep grazing area for the New England colonists.

Mariah raised her hand. "I was told that the Gungywamp means 'church of the people,' and that the structures there were built by Irish monks. The woman I spoke with called them Culdee monks."

The guide sighed heavily and rolled her eyes. She allowed her mike to swing by her side as she listened to Mariah's comments. "Miss, that is pure internet fantasy of the worse kind. I am sorry you were misinformed about this site. There is no evidence of Druidic or Celtic or Wiccan influences in the building of these structures at Gungywamp. There is absolutely nothing at Gungywamp that indicates any Pre-Columbian travelers here in North America, most certainly not in New England."

Mariah persisted. "But the woman I spoke with told me that there's a beehive shaped building there that lets the sun in on the equinox--you know, the way Newgrange outside of Dublin lets the sun in on the winter solstice."

"I'm sorry, miss, it's all nonsense! And I'll bet you were told that Gungywamp was a Celtic word?"

"Gaelic," Mariah corrected.

"More nonsense. Gungywamp is a Native American word!"

"What does it mean?" Mariah asked.

"The linguists are still working on the translation, but it's definitely Native American, most likely Algonquin." She shook her head in obvious frustration. "The Greyline tour operator should have told you that when you bought your ticket. The volunteer guides at the site are serious archeology students and professors, and they do not tolerate the perpetration of these kinds of rumors. If you're interested in new age fantasy, you can find it on the internet, not here. Here you'll find serious scientists."

Mariah felt her cheeks burning at the guide's chastising tone. She leaned back in her seat.

A woman near her in a black and purple quilted vest leaned across the aisle. "That was very rude of her," she told Mariah in a haughty tone. "What's more, she's wrong. These structures we'll see today are identical in style to many found in the British Isles and Ireland. There's plenty of evidence that pre-historic sailors from Ireland, Scotland, and Scandinavia came to America. Oh, these professor types and their near-worship of the Columbian records. As if no one dared to cross the Atlantic until Isabel and Ferdinand forked over the goods. Talk about your nonsense."

Mariah nodded, but instinctively pulled away. There was too much anger on this bus, from both the guide and from this passenger. "Excuse me," she said, pulling her phone from her pocket. "I need to make a phone call. I think I'll go to the back of the bus where it's less crowded."

She found an empty seat over a back wheel, and pulled out her cell. Turning it on for the first time in hours, she saw she had fourteen missed calls from her mother and three from her brother. There was another from a number she didn't recognize and she punched it to see if the unknown person had left a voice mail. "It's Craig, Mariah," the familiar voice of her godfather announced. "Call when you're ready."

Craig had known her mother long before Mariah was born, and in fact her mother had always credited him with getting her through her first difficult year of teaching. Craig seemed to be a steadying influence on her mother: she called him when she was feeling stressed and overwhelmed. One time when she was barely a teenager, Mariah overheard her father talking to

Dale out in the back yard where they thought she couldn't hear. "Do you ever get jealous of Sam talking to this guy Craig all the time?" Dale asked. "I mean they seem really close."

"No, Dale," Charlie said immediately, "they're not *that* close; Sam would never cheat on me. I know she wouldn't. And besides, Sam would have kicked my butt out of here more times than I can remember if she didn't have Craig to talk her down off the ledges, and that's a fact. Sure I wish I could do that for her, but I can't sometimes. We're both lucky to have him as a friend."

Mariah didn't know what that meant back then. She didn't want to know. She tried to forget she'd ever heard it, but she never could. She thought of it now as she punched the recall button on her phone. She bet Craig could talk her down too.

"Mariah!" Craig's voice rang out across the phone. "So good to hear from you!"

"I'm happy to hear your voice too," she said meekly.

"Where are you?"

"I'm on a Greyline tour bus on my way to Gungywamp."

"Gungywamp!!" he exclaimed. "What is that? Some kind of summer camp from a Goosebumps novel?"

"Maybe that's the next story I'm going to hear!" she said with a laugh. "Everybody seems to agree that this Gungywamp place is a site where Native Americans lived, and after them English colonists. And somewhere along the line somebody built these stone structures shaped like bee hives. But some people here think these stone buildings were built by--"

"Very big bees?" Craig interjected.

"No!" she exclaimed then she paused. "Maybe that's what the Goosebumps story will be about."

175

"Maybe you're going to write a Goosebumps story," Craig said. "Maybe that's what this journey is all about. Maybe you're going to become a writer of fantasy stories for tweens."

"Stop making me laugh!" she squealed, and suddenly she felt like crying, realizing how serious she'd been for weeks now, ever since her father died. It felt good to laugh again. "I want to finish my story," she said softly.

"Okay, I'll try not to interrupt."

"Some people here think the stone structures were built by Irish monks who came to New England--well, long before it was New England--because they were chased from their homes by Viking invaders. And they built these structures as places for meditation and worship."

"That resonates," Craig said simply.

"Do you think that's true?" she asked.

"It's certainly possible."

"Yes," she continued, "but other people think that's a load of bull, and they make no bones about saying so, right to your face! They say there's no scientific evidence. They say these structures were built by Native Americans or by English colonists as places to shear their sheep or use as root cellars."

"That makes sense too."

"But what resonates with you?" she asked.

"What resonates is that it doesn't matter," he conceded.

"But this woman told me a wonderful story about the monks and then this science girl took it away!"

"Mariah," Craig said intently, "there is nothing in the universe apart from God. As for your two stories, they're both very interesting, they're both logical, and either one might be true. Maybe both of them are true. But what does it matter? Everything we experience here on the earth realm is illusion; none of it is real. The only reality is God. God is having a dream that she is seven billion people. And when God wakes up it won't matter if those people were Irish monks or colonial sheepherders. What matters is that we can wake up--inside the dream--we can wake up! Don't get caught up in other people's reality, in other people's drama. Stay focused on the divine essence that is inside every cell in your body."

"But how do I do that?"

"Everything you've experienced thus far has prepared you for this moment. You designed this experience so you could learn from it. You even called me to be here for you to talk to about it. Now all you have to do is trust your own heart. You are divine essence!"

Mariah smiled sadly. "You sound like my dad," she whispered.

"Mariah," Craig continued, "why is this thimble so important to you?"

"Well," Mariah hesitated, not wanting to sound uncertain or self-deprecating the way she had when Geneva asked this same question. "I've been giving that question a lot of thought," she said stiffly. "It's hard to articulate, but I think it has to do with family loyalty. With wanting to take my rightful place as a mature member of the Easter family."

"Right," Craig said in a curt tone.

Mariah sensed doubt in her godfather's brief retort. "The Easter family thimble represents our legacy," she said emphatically. "It's been handed down for 150 years!"

"And it's engraved with a red-tailed hawk," Craig said.

"Yes, exactly," Mariah exclaimed, sitting up in her seat.

"Not just one hawk—two hawks! Craig, I feel so drawn to these hawks. Hawks have been coming to me—in the waking world and in my dreams. And here on this thimble there are two identical hawks. Twin hawks!"

"Do you realize how much passion you feel when you speak about the hawks, Mariah?" Craig asked her. "This is what your journey is about, not family legacy and loyalty. The hawks bring an energy that is beckoning you, that you can't resist."

"Craig, did you know I had a twin?" Mariah asked. "A twin who died before I was born?"

"Yes, I knew that, Mariah. I was there. I took your mother to the hospital the night she had to have her Fallopian tube removed."

Mariah was silent, wondering why that had had to happen, wishing her twin could have been with her now on this bus. "I don't understand, Craig! That thimble belongs with me. I'm the one who has a connection to it. How could someone else even dare to touch it? How could someone take it away from me?"

Craig voice was steady. "Sometimes," he said, "we manifest what we fear most."

Mariah switched to a whisper, lest anyone else on the bus overhear her crying. "It's not fair," she blurted, knowing she could not control the husky intensity of her voice. "I do the best I can to think positive. To manifest good things. But, Craig, my father died. . ." She broke off, choking up, sniffling and weeping.

"Sometimes," Craig said gently, "we manifest what we fear most so we can project it outside of ourselves, so we can look it in the face. And then we realize that we have the courage and the compassion we need to love ourselves through it."

Mariah was quiet for a long time considering his words. "Mariah," she heard him say softly. "Are you still there?"

"I'm here."

"You know your mother is feeling very tired and sad. She wants to go home. Can you talk to her now?"

"She's there with you?" Mariah asked, suddenly excited.

"Well, I think it's more accurate to say I'm here with her and Dale. I'm in the van with them and we're driving to Mystic, Connecticut, to find you. We're pretty close now--what's that? Dale says we've less than a hundred miles to go."

"Me too!" Mariah said. "I'm almost there! Oh, yes, please, Craig, put my mom on the phone."

"Mariah!" Samantha exclaimed, her voice cracking.

"Oh, Mom, please don't cry," Mariah begged. "I'm so sorry I hurt you, but this was something I needed to do."

"Maybe there's a purpose," Samantha conceded. "Craig's here, and soon we'll be close enough to go see Luisa and Anna."

"I'd like that," Mariah told her.

"Please keep your phone on Mariah. We'll be together soon!"

***

Dale, Samantha and Craig drove up to the antique store in Mystic that advertised the Easter family thimble for sale. "Hey, this is a nice place," Dale said, sounding surprised.

"The other places weren't so nice?" Craig asked.

"The first one was okay," Samantha told him, "but it was in this dingy strip mall. That last place though--" she shivered a bit in melodramatic fashion. "It was a real dive, and the owner

179

was a troll."

"Exactly!" Dale exclaimed. "I think he really was a troll. He was mean too."

Craig laughed. "I think you all have landed in some strange fairy tale here."

They got out of the van, and Samantha bent down to smell the plants growing in a window box outside the shop. "Lavender!" she exclaimed. "So beautiful, can you smell that? Heavenly."

Craig smiled as Samantha plucked off a sprig and handed it to him. "See how your mood has changed now that you've let go of your fears?"

She grit her teeth. "I've still got a little bit of fear I'm holding in reserve in my back pocket here," she confessed. She pointed up the street. "Oh look--crocuses! We don't see those that often on the west coast--so tiny and sweet." She strolled up half a block to get a better look.

Dale leaned in toward Craig. "I'm glad you came out," he said. "My dad always said you could talk Sam down off the ledges."

"No," Craig said, shaking his head with a smile. "I remind Samantha that the ledge doesn't actually exist. She does the rest herself."

Samantha came back to them, glancing at her watch. "Should we go inside or wait for Mariah?"

"I hate to be a pessimist," Dale said, "but I think we better go inside and make sure that thimble is really here--and if it is here, we better snatch it up fast before someone is able to steal it away again."

Craig and Samantha nodded their agreement. Dale led the way. A bell clattered as they went through the door.

The shop looked like an expensive jewelry store, seeming to specialize in antique settings. Rows and rows of sterling silver tea services and flatware were laid out in glass cases on one side of the room. The rest of the store was filled with rings, brooches, necklaces, and earrings.

The woman at the counter looked like she'd stepped out of a hair care ad from the 60s with a platinum blonde pageboy hair do and cat's eye glasses. Nonetheless she was young and stunning in a white blouse and a pencil thin black skirt. "Can I help you?" she asked in a pleasant but high-pitched voice.

Dale held out a page he'd printed from the website showing a photo of the thimble. "We've come to purchase this thimble," he said.

She barely looked at the picture. "I'm sorry sir, but we have no thimbles here."

"But isn't this the name of your store here on this ad?" Dale stated as if he had the poor woman on the witness stand. "This is the name and address matching the inscription painted on your plate glass window. Take a look at this ad, miss, and tell me why you think you don't carry thimbles!"

She looked a little shaken at his insistence, though Craig looked like he might laugh at loud. Samantha touched Dale's forearm as if preventing him from jumping down the young woman's throat. The sales woman took the page cautiously from Dale as if handling an explosive. "Sir, this has our name and address, that's true, but this isn't our phone number or email address. This is a bogus advertisement, sir."

"Oh my God," Samantha lamented. "I can't believe someone would do this!'

Dale stepped closer to the sales clerk, and assumed an even pushier tone. "Has this ever happened before? Do you know of anyone who would like to discredit or defraud your business? Have there been any suspicious looking characters in or around your shop in the last week or so?"

"No, I don't know, I don't know what to say," the young woman said stepping back from the counter. "I'm very sorry, if you come back tomorrow you can speak with my aunt; she's the owner here, but she won't be back until tomorrow. What can I say? I'm just sorry, okay?"

"I'm sure it's not your fault," Samantha said in a reassuring voice, though she herself looked ready to cry again. "Dale," she said insistently, "let's go."

He pulled his arm away from her. "But umm--" he shook his head, conceding she was right. "I'm sorry," he said. "I'm stunned."

The woman stepped back toward the counter. "Okay," she said slowly, giving her shoulders a tiny shrug. Her eyes darted away, unsure what to do next. "Have a nice day," she said meekly, addressing her own hands.

Craig burst out laughing at this. "Thank you!" he exclaimed. "You have a nice day too."

They shuffled out to the sidewalk and Samantha elbowed Craig in the ribs. "I know, I know," Samantha gushed. "Perry Mason here cracked you up."

"What?" Dale said innocently, and Craig continued to laugh.

"What are we going to do now?" Samantha asked no one in particular.

Craig shook his head. "I got nothing," he said. "I'm just along for the ride."

"Well," Dale said, "this is where Mariah is coming; maybe we should give her a call."

"And tell her the thimble is missing again?" Samantha exclaimed. "I don't think so!"

"No," Dale agreed. "We don't want to tell her about the thimble. But we want to track her progress."

Craig already had his phone out. "Use mine," he offered Samantha, and she took it gratefully and punched in Mariah's number.

"She's not answering," Samantha said, nearly shrieking. "What is the matter with that girl! I told her to leave her phone on!"

"Maybe it's running out of juice," Craig said.

"Oh, my God, you're right! I should have told her to leave it off to save the battery."

"Sam," Dale said. "Stop second guessing yourself. Look, we know Mariah's coming. Let's sit down and wait."

Craig pointed toward a Krispy Krème in the center of the block. "I'll get us some donuts."

Chapter Fourteen

The tour bus turned into the Gungywamp grounds and Mariah got off the bus for the guided tour. The heavy set woman who had practically proclaimed herself a Druid wheedled though the crowd to stand next to her. "Wait'll you see the stone structures," she told Mariah, "you'll see they have a sacred purpose. You can feel it, the energy is so strong."

The sky was cloudy and the air cool so Mariah pulled her cloak out of her pack. The Druidic woman stood uncomfortably close, and Mariah could almost feel the woman's eyes on her as she struggled with one hand to pull the drawstring close. "Easter," the woman said.

"What?" Mariah asked, startled.

"It says Easter on the cosmetic bag in your back pack. That's sweet--your favorite holiday?"

"It's my name," Mariah said, trying to sound matter of fact and dismissive.

"Your name!" the woman exclaimed. "How special--your parents named you Easter? Or did you dub yourself with that name?"

Mariah swallowed hard, embarrassed by this unwanted attention. "Easter is my last name," she said reluctantly, now hoping the woman would leave her alone.

"Your last name! So you are of the Easter family! Oh glory be! You are descended from the offspring of the Vernal Equinox Goddess, the Goddess of rebirth and resurrection. Coming here to the church of the people will be a homecoming for you, Ms Easter. Welcome home."

Mariah drew back in shock, glancing around to see if anyone was looking but everyone was more interested in navigating the uneven terrain that led to the stone structures. "Okay," she murmured to the Druid, giving her a curt nod. She pulled the cloak over her shoulders and immediately she felt calmer. The woman was stepping ahead of her on the trail, as Mariah pulled the hood up to cover the crown of her head. Just then the Druid looked back at Mariah, and Mariah saw the woman's face go blank. Her head darted back and forth as if looking for something in the crowd. Then the woman shrugged and walked away from her. Mariah felt relieved.

They hiked on until they came to a large room dug into the ground lined with stone. "This room was used as a root cellar or a shelter to shear sheep--perhaps both at different times with different occupants," the guide was saying. Mariah stood at the back of the crowd, nodding and taking it all in. It was interesting, all the stories were interesting, but it was not her story. Neither was the story of the Vikings in Minnesota nor the Native peoples in Arizona. Her story was of family loyalty and being true to self. Here at Gungywamp was a story of occupancy and ownership and an argument of who would claim both.

"Notice this smoke hole back here," the guide said, pointing. "It was used for--"

"That is no smoke hole!" the Druid woman shouted at the guide. "That is an astrological vent to signal the equinox in the church of the people!"

"There is absolutely no evidence to substantiate that claim, ma'am," the guide said in a singsong voice. "But thank you for sharing."

"Aren't you even going to allow us to go inside?" the Druid exclaimed.

"No, ma'am," the guide said in her bored detached tone. "This is a fragile archeological site. We cannot take the chance of allowing a multitude of people to traipse through such a vulnerable dwelling."

"You are denying the church to its people and the people to their church," the Druid shouted. "Where's Ms Easter? I know she'll agree with me." She stood on tiptoe and swept her gaze across the crowd. Mariah pulled her cloak closer across her face and the woman couldn't seem to find her. For a moment Mariah wondered if the cloak was indeed magical. It seemed to bestow invisibility! She stifled a laugh, crossed her arms and breathed deeply.

The crowd chuckled and the Druid woman squealed but said nothing more. The guide led the group on. Bringing up the rear, Mariah paused to stare down at the stone lined room. It was beautifully made, no matter who actually made it.

Alone now as the tour headed up a sloping trail, Mariah heard a low humming. Surprised, she leaned forward in curiosity. Was someone singing? No, it seemed someone was laughing. She inched closer to the edge of the rope line that barred tourists from advancing toward the sunken room. Planting her boots firmly on the muddy surface, she bent down to get a better look. Her spine tingled as the snickering twisted into a high-pitched cackle. Mariah froze, tempted to back off. Steeling herself, she moved closer, slowly stepping over the low rope and squatting to look inside. She caught sight of something that made her jerk back, clutching the vulnerable spot between her breasts. There in the stone structure perched Pale-woman, the monster who had assaulted her mother and stolen the thimble on the day of her father's funeral in Sacramento.

Mariah stood in shock, not thinking, suddenly panting, overwhelmed with a frantic desire for she knew not what. Bracing herself, she stepped forward again.

Pale-women seemed oblivious to Mariah's presence. She perched undisturbed and upright in her tight black garments. Her skin shimmered as if under water. She leaned back against the stones, her arms folded lightly across her chest. She coughed slightly and her right hand moved slowly forward to touch her mouth. Covering Pale-woman's right index finger was a tiny cap of gold. Mariah saw it and gasped. It was her thimble.

Mariah stuffed her fist into her mouth to keep from shouting out. The woman seemed to be waiting for something or someone but Mariah couldn't imagine who or what. "Is she waiting for me?" she whispered to herself, and the tiny scratch of her vocal cords attracted unwanted attention. The woman's gaze inched up her way. Pale-woman seemed to be staring right at her, yet not registering any recognition of a human form standing just yards away. Mariah felt her heart would burst out of her throat but she didn't dare move.

Pale-woman was basking in the fading afternoon light that streamed into the smoke hole. She lifted her head, and again looked toward Mariah. With a small satisfied smile, she scampered out of the hole. Throwing back her shoulders, she strode toward the trail, passing within inches of Mariah's face and hands.

Mariah's anxious limbs could stay still no longer. Pale-woman was getting away with her thimble! This was no coincidence. She had been brought here for a purpose. Her toes curled in her leather boots and she started running. She felt the cool moist air against her face, heard the hard slap of her new leather boots against the dirt. She screamed and launched herself off the ground toward Pale-woman's back. She felt her cloak sweep back, revealing her face and form, as Pale-woman glanced back. Mariah reveled in the anguished, open mouth, the expanding white eyes--the horrified look of shock Pale-woman displayed—a split second before Mariah landed on her back, knocking her to the ground.

Mariah had never felt so strong before. She lay on top of the woman's head and shoulders, pushing her face into the rocky trail. "Give me the thimble," she screeched. "Give me *my* thimble."

Pale-woman screamed. Her arms were splayed out before her and the thimble was exposed. Mariah crawled up the woman's back, reaching, reaching, grasping for the thimble on Pale-woman's right index finger. Pale-woman screeched like some kind of a wolf/leopard hybrid, yowling and baying, her animalistic vocalizations peppered with obscenities.

Mariah was nearly there, she could almost reach the thimble, but as she crept, she shifted much of her weight off Pale-woman's back. Pale-woman rolled, and Mariah tried to roll with her, but it was too late. She had lost her leverage. Pale-woman sprang to her feet. Mariah jumped up and the two women faced each other crouching and hissing.

Mariah was unprepared for this kind of combat, but she breathed deeply. She focused on the thimble. Finally feeling ready she took a tentative step forward, tilting back as if to kick Pale-woman in the teeth. Pale-woman lurched down, ready to grab Mariah's leg, to knock her off balance. But Pale-woman had fallen for a ruse: Mariah had lured her in close. Mariah grabbed a fistful of white hair, then ran the fine sharp new heel of her leather boot against Pale-woman's shin. Pale woman squealed, and bent instinctively. The thimble tumbled off her finger and Mariah snatched it up.

Immediately Mariah stuffed the thimble down inside her bra and backed away. Her cloak fell over her shoulders and chest as she crossed her arms to protect her breasts. Pale-woman stood confused, looking this way and that, apparently unable to see Mariah under her magic cloak. Mariah watched in astonishment as Pale-woman wailed with a terrifying resonance. Then the otherworldly creature turned and disappeared in a burst of flame.

Mariah stood stiff and still, panting again, unsure whether she would laugh or cry. The sun had fallen below the horizon and the sky was quickly darkening. She jogged a short way up the trail where she thought the tour group had gone. It was deserted, dark and getting darker.

The frantic whir of a hummingbird's wings caught her attention. The bird was a tiny burst of scarlet and green in the fading light. She scrambled to follow it, but it disappeared as she came to the edge of the sunken stone structure. A wind came up, pressing against her shoulders and cheeks. She leapt down into the pit, seeking shelter.

She pulled out her cell phone. She had missed seven more calls from her mother. She had no bars out here in the wilderness. At least her phone provided a tiny bit of light in the darkness, as she huddled in the ancient dwelling and prepared to spend the night.

***

In Mystic, Samantha and Craig sat silently on separate double beds in a room at the Marriott Hotel. Samantha clutched her rosary and stared into space. Craig perused the room service menu. "There are three different restaurants to choose from if we go downstairs," Craig said. "But they have a pretty good selection up here too."

"I'm not hungry," Samantha told him.

"Samantha, you've got to eat something before room service closes down, or you'll end up eating from the mini bar in the middle of the night. That'll cost you."

Samantha riveted her stare at her long time friend. "I'm a millionaire now, remember?" she said. "So if I want to eat an

$18 jar of macadamia nuts at 3 am, that's what I'm going to do." Her mouth twisted into a bitter knot. "Too bad I didn't take out an insurance policy on my daughter too!" she lamented, and then she started to cry.

"Okay," Craig said, swinging his legs around to lean over and touch her hand. "Now you're buying into the drama. Cut it out, and let's get something to eat."

"But I'm not--"

"You haven't had anything but a sugar donut in the last five hours, Samantha. How bout a hamburger--I can order you a hamburger when I order me a hamburger, okay?"

Samantha started to cry again and Craig passed her a box of Kleenex.

When Mariah didn't show at the antique store and didn't answer her cell phone, they had called the police. The police officers were polite, but implied that Mariah was most likely a run-away, and certainly not a top priority for their search and rescue units. "Let us know when she's been missing three days, ma'am," the officer had said.

"She has been missing three days," Samantha had pleaded. "She's been missing ever since we left Minnesota--"

"But you said you spoke with her by cell phone this morning, ma'am. That doesn't count as missing in my book. Sorry, ma'am, but in my experience, she'll be calling as soon as she's hungry and the money has run out."

"You don't know my daughter, officer," Samantha said indignantly. But Craig took her arm and steered her away.

"Not to mention that she's not going to get all that hungry when she's riding on Charlie's credit card," he said.

"It's upsetting that you're being so flippant about this," Samantha whined.

"I'm not being flippant, Samantha. I'm seeing more clearly than you are right now," he told her. "I don't mean to be harsh, but right now Mariah is fine. I can see her, and she's okay. She's not exactly where she planned to be right now, but she's okay, all right?"

She leaned against him and he gave her a brotherly hug. Dale walked up with the officer's card in his hand. "They're going to keep an eye out, Samantha, but they won't start searching until tomorrow."

Samantha nodded. "Well," she had said, turning practical again, "I don't guess there's any point in us sleeping in the van tonight. Let's go find a hotel." At that, she had pulled out her own credit card and had had Dale reserve three rooms at the nicest hotel in the area.

***

Samantha blew her nose, then threw a wadded up tissue toward a wastebasket near the bathroom door. It missed. "Craig," she began slowly, "do you really think I manifested this evil woman who stole the thimble?

Craig winced. "What?"

"You said my family was Irish so I was the only one who could have manifested a banshee. Or were you joking?"

Craig sighed. "Listen to your own words, Samantha. Do I think you manifested an evil woman to steal your daughter's thimble? I don't know. Do you think this thief was truly evil? Do you think she truly was a banshee? These are questions you have to answer. I can't answer them for you."

Samantha stared down at her hands, blinking back tears, feeling scolded. "You must be really hungry, huh?" she asked meekly.

Craig laughed. "Samantha, what I do know is this:

anything that you attract--that you perceive to be bad or evil or oppressing—it is only a projection of your own fears."

"Fear." Samantha spat out the word. "And what's left for me to be afraid of, now that I've lived through my husband's death?"

Craig took her hand in his. "Oh, we both know there's something much worse."

She looked into his eyes. "If something ever happened to Mariah. . ."

"Samantha," he said firmly, "you didn't choose this, and yet you drew this experience to you to push back spiritual boundaries, to expand your own and the collective consciousness."

"But how do I do that?" she asked, her voice desperate.

"Don't worry about how," Craig said, spreading his hands. "How will take care of itself. Just hang on and enjoy the ride."

Samantha shrugged, spreading her own hands in a gesture of surrender. "But what should I do now?"

"Now? Well, right now you should let the Craig vehicle call room service and order something to eat." As he picked up the phone, there was a knock at the door. "Wow, I didn't even have to call them," he said. "This place is good."

"I'm sure that's Dale," Samantha said, smiling a little. "Open the door."

Craig got up and Dale came in. "Hey, how are you?" he asked Samantha cautiously.

"As well as can be expected," Samantha said, fingering the box of tissues.

"Look," he said slowly. "I've got some news. I hope this

doesn't upset you."

"About Mariah?" Samantha said frantically, half jumping off the bed.

"Oh, God, no," Dale said. "Something else--sorry, I didn't mean to be so mysterious."

"What is it?" Samantha asked, her voice still high pitched and anxious.

"Well, I was messaging with Luisa, and she felt so bad for you that she wants to come see you right away. Tonight. She and her mom are on their way."

"Really? They're coming all this way tonight?"

"Yeah, in fact they should be here in about twenty minutes or so."

Samantha sat up then and noticed that Dale had showered and shaved and put on a shirt she didn't recognize; he'd probably bought it in a shop downstairs. "You look nice," she said with a wistful smile.

"Really?"

Samantha laughed. "Yes, of course, really!" She turned to Craig. "Guess we better get ready for guests too." She shrugged, looking at Dale. "It's good they're coming. It'll take my mind off missing Mariah."

***

The two families agreed to eat at the supper club on the ground floor of the hotel. Anna called Samantha's room when they'd arrived and were seated. "We're all here, Samantha-- Luisa and I--and I've brought Rafael too. I don't think you've ever met my son. You know he's almost 18 now."

"Anna, I'm so happy you're here," Samantha said.

"We've come to support you and Dale--and it'll be so good to see Craig again too," Anna said.

"We'll be down in a few minutes," Samantha said.

"Take your time, dear," Anna said simply. "And just think: tomorrow night we'll all be together at my house and Mariah will be dining with us too."

"Oh, Anna," Samantha said her voice nearly breaking, "thank you."

She saw Dale take a deep breath as she hung up the phone. "They're here," she said simply, and both she and Craig looked to Dale. He nodded with his whole upper body, as if psyching himself up to join in a football game when the team was on their own five-yard line. "I'm ready!" he said as he stood up.

Craig and Samantha flanked him as they walked into the dining room. Samantha saw Anna and her children sitting at a corner table overlooking a lit garden. Anna smiled broadly and waved. Samantha touched Dale's arm to point out the table to him. She saw Luisa sitting beside her mother: she was 28 now, at the peak of her beauty, her hair shimmering as the low light reflected on the natural blonde streaks that ran through her dark brown hair. She saw as Luisa's eyes landed on Dale that the young woman began to rock. Her mouth dropped open and she lifted her right hand to stim against her own face, her open palm striking her cheek and lips repeatedly in rapid succession as she moaned and wailed with increasing volume. Samantha swallowed hard watching her. Obviously Luisa had had little success controlling these tremors that she'd had since childhood. She looked over at Dale to gauge his reaction, but he was already darting away from her side. She was startled to see him stride up to Luisa's chair, kneel at her feet and forcefully take Luisa's hands in his.

"Luisa," he said in a warm tone, "Luisa." He rocked with her until she quieted, finally standing again to kiss her on the top of her head, then on her forehead and finally her cheek.

"I'm so happy to finally meet you in person, Luisa. So happy." Luisa leaned back and looked at his face, breathing deeply and nodding calmly.

Samantha stopped walking, stunned at the poignancy of the scene. She felt Craig rest his hand on her shoulder. "I wish you could see the energy potential that's manifesting," he whispered. "It's truly remarkable."

"Don't worry," she told him. "I see it."

Samantha looked then to her old friend, Anna. Luisa's mother had risen from her seat, her face a mixture of relief and enchantment. Blinking back tears, she turned toward Samantha, spreading her arms wide to welcome the family.

Chapter Fifteen

Mariah slept fitfully on the dirt floor of the stone structure. As the hours ticked by she reluctantly turned off the light of her cell phone in order to preserve its battery. In pitch-blackness now, she wrapped herself in her cloak and reached up under her sweater to pull out the thimble from inside her bra. She fit it over her right index finger, and somehow felt protected.

In the morning, in the grey light just before dawn, Mariah could see the silhouetted bodies of two hawks perched in twin pine trees near the opposing corners of the shelter. The birds seemed to be standing sentry. She held her breath when she saw them, astonished at their presence. As she sat up they stretched their wings too, looked about them and nodded to each other. In unison it seemed they turned to her. She looked from one to the other, and each seemed to meet her gaze. With a nod to the larger one she stood and they took off gliding above the trail. She collected her belongings, stashing her phone in her pocket and tucking her thimble back in her bra. Then she raced after the hawks.

The hawks led her to a highway, then soared to the left. She watched carefully for breaks in the sparse traffic then ran across the road and followed in the direction they seemed to point her. She was tired, sore, and hungry, but feeling very satisfied.

She hiked for several miles along the side of the road, unsure if she were heading toward Mystic or away from it. She was tempted to hitchhike, but she didn't dare. Her parents had always warned her against it. After beating Pale-woman, she knew she could face anything. Still there was a feeling deep inside that prevented her from sticking out her thumb.

She glanced at her cell phone occasionally to check the time. It was nearing 9 am, and she'd passed nothing but farmland and grazing grass. She felt discouraged and exhausted, fantasizing about the waffles her father used to make on Sunday mornings, served with pure New England maple syrup. He ordered some online nearly every month. This month from Vermont, next month from New Hampshire, even got some from Maine once. He used to do funny accents from every state in the northeast. Nobody else in California seemed to know--or care for that matter--that there was a different accent in Vermont than in New Hampshire or Maine. Bostonians of course spoke in a way that was unrivaled by anyone else in America, and Charlie could mimic them all. Mariah smiled thinking of it.

Around the bend came a Greyhound bus and as she watched it approach she felt a sense of destiny--even family legacy. She imagined her father's vagabond days: if it was true he would ask bus drivers to pull over and drop him off at random spots, well, maybe he also picked unconventional places to hop aboard. She decided to take a chance. She stood on the side of the road and waved her arms like crazy. The bus pulled over.

"Are you headed toward Mystic?" she asked.

"That's one of our stops, though we won't get there till late this afternoon," the driver informed her.

"It's that far?"

"No, we're a local; we've got to make a lot of stops before we can rest tonight," the man said sounding vaguely like a Robert Frost poem. "But you're welcome," he added. "We've got plenty of empty seats."

197

Mariah climbed aboard gladly, took a seat near the front and promptly fell asleep.

She awoke at the first stop, and in the 15-minute layover she bought a half dozen packets of peanut butter crackers from a vending machine along with an Almond Joy bar. It didn't satisfy her the way her dad's waffles would have, but it was enough for now. She stared out the window and wondered how often her father had traveled this road.

At the second stop she tried to call her mother but her phone was dead. She felt guilty that she hadn't called sooner. She noticed two hawks perched on fence posts along the side of the road. Were they the same guardian-hawks? Were they escorting her?

At the third stop she promised herself she'd find a pay phone, but the stop was nothing more than a bench by the side of the road. Men got out and rushed down to hide behind a row of bushes. Women were directed to a portajohn on the other side. Mariah crossed her legs and decided to wait.

At three fifteen in the afternoon, they rolled into Mystic. She thanked the driver and hastened out to the sidewalk to get her bearings. She was surprised to see a phone booth sitting in the middle of the sidewalk a half block down near an alley. So happy was she that she began to laugh, then tears were streaming down her cheeks. She ran to the anachronistic little steel building, and without hesitation she stepped inside.

As soon as she crossed the narrow threshold, a bony pale hand reached around her throat and she felt a cold metal blade against her skin. "Don't move," a raspy voice whispered. "I'll have the thimble whether you're dead or alive. Pull it out now."

She hadn't realized how tall Pale-women was and Mariah gasped with fear as the powerful figure towered over her. "Please--" she blurted.

"Just give it to me," she screeched.

"I will, I promise. Please, give me some space so I can move. It's inside my--inside my clothing."

The woman loosened her hold, dropping her hand down to Mariah's chest and Mariah could see that she had indeed been holding a sharp blade to her throat. She had no choice now. She reached inside her bra and pulled out the thimble. It was shiny and beautiful. She grasped it tightly with all five fingers of her right hand as she stared at the twin hawks engraved in its golden splendor. She wanted to drink it in, memorize it, because she was sure that she would never set eyes upon it again. She had searched long and hard, she had proved herself a worthy opponent, but she would surrender now. Nothing was more important than delivering herself back to her mother and brother who would both be crushed with sorrow without her. She tightened her fist around it. "Please put away your knife, and I'll give you the thimble. I'll let you have it. I won't search for it anymore," she said.

"Ha ha!" Pale-woman squealed in delighted victory as she clicked her switchblade closed though she still held Mariah tight. "Drop it in my hand," she rasped and Mariah complied.

Pale-woman held the thimble in her palm. "This is my family," she whispered as she closed her fist around it.

"What are you talking about?" Mariah challenged. "This belongs with *my* family."

"How little you understand," Pale-woman barked.

"What do you mean?" Mariah persisted, but Pale-woman released her then with a rough shove out of the booth. Holding the thimble high in victory Pale-woman stepped onto the sidewalk herself. Instantly two hawks swooped down upon her, piercing her white skin with beaks and talons. Mariah stepped back in horror, sheltering herself in the phone booth as the two birds worked their terror on Pale-woman. Pale-woman screamed in anguish at their savageness, and Mariah felt a swell of pity opening in her solar plexus. Who was this stranger? She had just declared a claim to the Easter family thimble: were they somehow related? Was she a projection of her own fears, as Craig had implied? Was she a piece of her soul?

Pale-woman dropped to the ground, her arm raised over her head to shield herself, but the raptors were relentless. They dug at her cheeks and her eyelids; they slashed her throat. "Stop!" Mariah screamed frantically. She stepped out of the booth and waved her arms to shoo the birds away. She realized she would need to reach in and attempt to grab the birds, but Pale-woman was falling backwards. Her fist curled open. The thimble rolled onto the pavement and its golden color shone in the fading afternoon light.

The birds abandoned the bleeding woman to bow before the thimble. The tiny object began to grow and shift into pulsing energy, pure light. Mariah couldn't look away. The thimble mutated into a swirling mass slowly solidifying into a golden-feathered bird, a hawk, smaller yet more brilliant than the sentries that greeted it. The newly formed creature stretched its wings, twisting its neck to examine its feathers first on the left, then the right. The other two hawks bowed their heads in a deferential display. The golden bird nodded in reply, then all three suddenly shot into the air. They flew above the road, then circled back to bow before Mariah. Startled, Mariah knew instinctively she must bow in return. The birds, seeming satisfied, took flight in a sudden burst of flame, popping in the air like fireworks on the fourth of July. Mariah stood amazed on the sidewalk, watching them soar until they were no longer visible.

Turning her eyes toward earth she was stunned to find herself on an empty street: no phone booth, no bleeding pale woman on the sidewalk at her feet. She turned rapidly from side to side: she was alone. Feeling self-conscious, she patted at her pockets, swept at her shoulders and hips as if brushing off sand or nightmares. She remembered how her mother, brother, and aunt--even Dale's mother--had spoken of her father as if he were mentally ill, suffering from some form of dementia. At this moment she couldn't help but feel a bit of fear at what she had just experienced, wondering if she too might be crazy. Had any of it been real? It came to her then that she had always known that there had been something a little different about her father; but she hadn't wanted to think about it. She hadn't wanted to face it. She liked to think that he was a magical creature, a rare blessed spirit that would live forever. And he would live forever--in her heart.

She looked up then and saw she stood in front of an Anna Victoria Pie Shop--one of the chain shops owned by her mother's dear friend. She laughed, thinking, this was exactly what she was hungry for--an Anna Victoria chicken potpie, with a piece of lemon meringue pie for dessert. She knew she still had her father's credit card to buy herself a good meal, but when she saw her mother she would surrender the card. It was time for her to pay her own way in the world.

She stepped inside, noting immediately that the shop was nearly empty, being as it was smack dab between lunch and dinner hours. She could hear voices in the back, and she craned her neck looking for the wait staff, wondering if she should search the restaurant for help.

"Mariah!" she heard a familiar voice exclaim. There was her mother running toward her, laughing and crying at the same time. She rushed forward to embrace her, to cry gratefully on her shoulder.

"Mariah," her mother whispered. "Are you all right?"

"Oh, Mommy," Mariah said, retreating into girlhood for a moment. "I have so much to tell you. I found the thimble."

Samantha leaned back to look at her daughter's face. "Did you, Mariah? But how--?"

Mariah shook her head. "It doesn't matter. It's gone now."

Samantha pulled her back into her arms. "Oh, my God, what a roller coaster for you!" She paused then asked in a very small voice, "Are you still searching for it?"

Mariah leaned back and shook her head. "You can stop worrying, Mom. I know the thimble is gone this time." She took a deep breath. "You see, I saw the thimble turn into a hawk."

Samantha raised her eyebrows. "Really? A hawk?"

Mariah laughed at her mother's attempt to treat her bizarre statement in a nonchalant manner. "I know, it sounds fantastic. But I saw it." She spread her hands. "Maybe the thimble was an enchanted shape shifter all along. Maybe our family worked some magic to release it from its spell. Or maybe—maybe I'm as crazy as Daddy was."

"Oh, no, Mariah," Samantha said, grasping her hand. "I never said your father was crazy. He was special; he was magical. Sometimes he had a hard time carrying all that magic inside him. But he was not crazy. Don't ever think your dad was crazy."

"I don't feel crazy either!" Mariah agreed. "But what I just saw was so outrageous. . ." She let her voice trail off, then she laughed, unsure if she was feeling exhilaration or anxiety. "I don't know what to think," she admitted. "What was that bird? What kind of power does it have?"

Samantha nodded slowly. "Mariah, I believe--and your father believed too—that each of us is on a journey through life. Each of us manifests many things along the way: some tangible, like chocolate chip cookies; some not so tangible, like laughter. Your father and I loved each other and we manifested you! You apparently manifested a hawk from a tiny gold thimble. Is it tangible? Is it an actual bird with feathers and claws--or is it a story? You're not even sure yourself. But what I do know is this: if you embark on your quest with an open heart, if your intention is to approach all creation with kindness, with faith that you will recognize the divine everywhere you go, then how can you help but manifest goodness?" She paused to touch her hand to her heart chakra. "At least that's what I believe."

Mariah hugged her mother again, feeling both satisfied and relieved. "Then I'll believe it too," she whispered.

"C'mon," Samantha said, taking Mariah's hand. "There are a lot of people who want to see you."

Samantha led her to the back of the restaurant, and they were all there, her own family. Dale was seated with his arm protectively around Luisa, who squealed and rocked as she punched the keys of an iPad. She touched Dale's cheek as she handed him the tablet to read. "Luisa says, 'I am so happy you are safe with us, Mariah. You are a lovely young woman now.'"

"Thank you, Luisa," Mariah murmured, though she wondered if Luisa heard her. She and Dale seemed to have eyes only for each other.

Anna was shouting a hearty welcome, and calling for the waiter to bring an extra chair. Craig was there too, giving her a knowing smile. "So how the hell are ya, Mariah?" he asked. "I'll bet you've got quite a story to tell."

"Oh, I don't know if it's worth telling," she said. "I feel kind of silly, that I put you all through this." She lowered her head, feeling herself blush. "I've given up on finding the thimble," she added suddenly. "I know it's gone for good this time."

"And there's a story in that too, isn't there?" Craig interjected, but Mariah shook her head quickly.

"No," she said. "I don't think so"

"Well, maybe it's not worth telling right now, but someday

I see you writing it," Craig told her.

Mariah looked at him with anticipation, curious at this new prediction, but her mother was taking her hand to direct her attention elsewhere.

"Mariah," Samantha said, "I want you to meet Rafael, Anna's son."

"Oh, yes," Mariah said, leaning forward to shake the young man's hand. "You were born in South America like Luisa, weren't you?"

"Yes, that's right," he said. "I lived there for the first three years of my life. Then my American mom brought me here to live with her and Luisa."

Mariah smiled, charmed by the golden brown eyes of this new stranger.

"Mariah," Samantha added, "we're all celebrating Rafa's birthday. He's 18 years old today!"

"Oh, happy birthday, Rafa!" Mariah said. "Guess I arrived right in time for some birthday pie!"

"But Mariah," her mother persisted, "don't you find that interesting--that Rafa is turning 18 today?"

Mariah gave her mother a blank stare. "I don't know; I guess," she said, then leaned close to Samantha. "What are you talking about?"

"Mariah! Don't you know today's date?"

Mariah took a deep breath and laughed. "Mom, I don't even know the day of the week right now! I guess I've been traveling so long that I'm all confused. So it's what--April something?"

"No!" Samantha blurted. "It's May 1st! Baby, it's your 18th

birthday too!"

Mariah stared at her mother in disbelief. "Really? It's May already? Really?" Then something occurred to her and she looked over at Rafa. "I guess we share a birthday," she said meekly, eyeing him more carefully.

"Maybe," he said with a mischievous glint in his eye. "Maybe we're actually twins!"

Mariah's mouth dropped open. "I was thinking the same thing," she said.

"This calls for another round of *Happy Birthday*," Dale said as he squeezed Luisa's shoulder.

"More candles!" Anna called to the waiter.

The evening light dimmed outside the restaurant's plate glass window. Three hawks flew toward the Mystic River.

THE END

ACKNOWLEDGEMENTS

Thank you to my late mother, who was indulgent enough to read me Peter Pan over and over and over again. I fell in love with stories and I fell in love with magic. Thanks to Craig, who actually was magic. And thanks to HC, who wasn't magic, but I forgive him for this.

Thank you, Universe, for all my family, friends and fellow writers who have supported and rooted for me: my brother, Andrew, my surrogate sister, Diane, my friends Leslie, June, John, Roxann, both Carols, Matt, Sue Mac, and lunch buddies Bernadette, Lyn, and Dena. And thank you, AngelCat, for being a wonderful companion and muse.

Thank you as well to the wonderful women of Wellspring Women's Center and the Franciscan Living Center, especially the Catholic sisters who help me make peace with The Church. Who would have guessed at this point in my life that I would encounter and befriend such congenial nuns? It is a great blessing!

ABOUT THE AUTHOR

Nancy Schoellkopf is the author of the critically acclaimed *Yellow-Billed Magpie,* a novel of spiritual promise, and the short story collection *Rover and Other Magical Tales.* She has been telling stories and writing poems for many lifetimes. It goes without saying that she's needed a second income, so this time around she happily taught amazing children in special education classes in two urban school districts in Sacramento, California. A full time writer now, she enjoys lavishing attention on her cats, her garden and her intriguing circle of family and friends. Contact her at her website: www.nancyschoellkopf.com

Manufactured by Amazon.ca
Bolton, ON

11590120R00122